A Life in Progress

and other short stories

Tracy Million Simmons

Chasing Tigers Press

This one is for Brenda.

*Your time was too short and you left a hole in our lives and our hearts
that we will fill with stories of your spirit, your love, and your kindness.*

Brenda Kay Schriner Million
October 11, 1958 – January 12, 2017

Published by Meadowlark, with Chasing Tigers Press
P.O. Box 333, Emporia, KS 66801
www.meadowlark-books.com

Thank you to www.alovelikethis.co
For permission to use the dedication photos of Brenda Million.

ISBN: 978-0-9966801-3-4

Library of Congress Control Number: 2017910265

A Life in

Progress

and other short stories

Tracy Million Simmons

A MEADOWLARK BOOK

Contents

Word Search

I seek words
at the bottom of the kitchen sink,
tucked among my nearly-sorted piles of bills and junk mail,
slipped between wrinkled folds of clean laundry,
hidden like so many mates to troublesome socks.

I chase words
across cracks of aged sidewalks,
through waves created by my own pin-wheeling arms,
as my feet thump-thump on the circling belt of a treadmill,
catching fleeting phrases when lucky.

I search for words
on the friendly pages of the internet,
inside the ink-filled marvel of a printed book,
beneath my eyelids where I peer as sleep overtakes me,
assured to remember those gems when day breaks again.

I find words
dripping from the ends of fingertips placed on keyboard,
flowing where pen meets page,
coming unbidden,
provided I remain still and not frighten them away.

TMS / December 2011

Glorious

Y ou should enter that sunflower in the county fair," said Iris Finnegan, Emma's neighbor in 204B.

"Why would I do that?" Emma knew she sounded cranky. "Fairs are for children."

But when she looked at her sunflower she had to admit that her heart swelled. It was huge, and it was glorious. She had poked that little seed into the soil and watched it grow, arching its pale little back from the surface and straightening to reach for the sun. Not only had she tended this beauty, she had tended its parents and grandparents, as well.

Emma had grown sunflowers for many seasons. Starting with numerous seedlings, she would pick and choose until she had selected the very best. Every day she would sing and talk to that chosen flower until it grew large and beautiful. She loved the way it swiveled its head in greeting to the sun. At the end of its season, she would collect every seed. Her apartment, in fact, was filled with the sunflower seeds not chosen. Bags marked by year were stuffed in every crevice: her panty drawer, the cookie jar, a high shelf in her closet, a tin can under the bathroom sink...

Kooky Old Emma Green.

Even Iris called her that.

Quirky. Crotchety. Downright mean. And crazy to boot.

The assortment of elderly at Sunnyside Acres Retirement Home assumed senility was her companion. Not so, Emma knew. She was no more addled now than she had been sixty-five years ago on the morning of her eighteenth birthday. She had more upstairs than most twenty years her junior.

How glorious eighteen had been. When she closed her eyes she could still remember her body as it was; firm, ripe, hard, yet soft in all the right places. She remembered pulling stockings on lean legs that walked, ran, and danced. She could almost believe she had the same jet-black, glossy mane she had tucked up under her brother's cap so many years ago.

Her hands were still strong. Gardening kept them from going soft. She never needed help. At least, not for simple things such as opening jars. Poor Iris was knocking on her door every other day, begging Emma to open this jar or that. Even Howard Wake, who had just moved in, down and across the walk from Emma's apartment, was known to ask for help because his hands were failing him. He had been a carpenter in his prime.

She had to admit, however, that Howard was one of her more pleasant neighbors. He may have been the only one who didn't call her names behind her back. Well, he did call her one name, but it was a name that Emma didn't mind much.

"There's my Sunflower Gal," he would say as they passed on the walk or, on a rare day, when Howard dawdled in the garden and inspected her plants.

It made her proud. She didn't much care whether most residents noticed her efforts in the garden—a supposed community effort—but few old folk, other than Emma, did more than take an occasional stroll. When Howard took the time to examine her tomato plants, run his hands along her marigolds, or marvel at her enormous sunflowers, she found herself cherishing the attention. She would even engage in his banter, asking what he thought of local city commission candidates or how he felt about the stoplight the city proposed be placed at the corner.

Maybe twenty years ago, she would have pursued a relationship with Howard. Forty years ago, certainly. She would have rung him up and asked him out for a meal. That's what modern women did when they were interested in a man. Honestly, that's what Emma would have done in her youth. She had been just that kind of girl.

That's what Edward had loved about her. "You're not afraid of anything," he would whisper to her as they cuddled under the sheets at night. It was hard to believe so much time had passed … and to think that Emma once believed her life was over when Edward died of a heart attack at the age of fifty-three. If she had only known how many years were left ahead of her.

Emma looked up into the face of her sunflower. She closed her eyes and felt the sun as she imagined the flower might, remembering herself in full bloom again. This sunflower was beginning to die. It was the cycle of things. This flower, her most impressive specimen to date, was nearing the end of its life. Emma sighed, thinking that it would be nice if everything ended so predictably.

Maybe she would invite Howard to help her plant sunflowers next year. It seemed like a lot of trouble to go to for two old people near the end of their seasons, but just to have someone to talk to...

Emma thought back to those first few years after Edward had gone. She missed him terribly, yet it was somewhat liberating to have a home all to herself. She could put down a book and know that it would still be there when she returned, no one to bury it under a pile. She never had to worry about going to the bathroom and finding the toilet paper roll empty.

Truthfully though, she wouldn't mind having a grandchild or two to run about and muck up the place. At this point, it would be great or even great-great grandchildren, Emma supposed, had Becky, her daughter and only child, lived to marry and have babies. Not a day went by that Emma failed to wish she could trade some of her own years for those her daughter was short.

Sometimes Emma thought that if she had only known how long it would last, she would have invited someone like Howard, or someone else from Sunnyside Acres, to help her plant flowers years ago. Maybe she would have even been nice to Iris and accepted her invitations to lunch. But who would have thought, way back then, that so many years remained ahead of her?

❋ ❋ ❋

"It's my Sunflower Gal!" Howard was making his way through the garden with his cane on a bright spring morning.

Emma busied herself digging trenches along the sidewalk. She was planting pansies this year, purple.

Howard stopped and inspected a peony bush not yet in bloom.

Emma swallowed, determined to greet him with a civil tongue. She mulled a few options in her head before she finally said, "Good morning, Howard. Wonderful weather, isn't it?"

Her giant sunflowers were growing nicely along the white picket fence. Emma had filled in the rest of the garden with clusters of color. She'd picked out a much larger variety than usual. Her special sunflower, the one she sang to each morning and tended with loving care, stood on its own near the water faucet so that she could keep a steady drip of moisture on it through the peak of its season. Indeed, it was already taller than the others by a good four inches. Its stalk was thicker and stronger, too. Emma chalked this up to the steady supply of food she gave it. Plants needed breakfast just as much as people did.

"I heard you singing this morning," Howard said.

Emma trenched a little more furiously and declined to reply. That was why they all thought she was crazy. They heard her singing each morning in the garden. Singing was not a crazy thing to do, but the fact that she sang to a single, particular sunflower… that was why they thought she was out of her head. She was an old woman who would sing to a plant, yet hardly spoke a word to most of her neighbors. She ate her breakfast each morning with a mammoth sunflower, yet refused invitations to lunch from even the most harmless of old ladies living in proximity. They didn't know that she also shared her breakfast with the sunflowers. No one had pulled the dirt back to see where she had tucked bits of breakfast cereal and toast to nourish her sunflower's roots.

❊ ❊ ❊

Howard was at her door early. She watched him from the slit in her window curtain for a moment before double-checking that the buttons on her blouse were matched evenly with their holes and answering the door.

"What do you want?" Her voice came out much sharper than she intended. She tried again. "How are you this morning? Can I help you?"

"I was just thinking of taking a stroll through the garden, Emma. Thought you might want to come along."

She liked the way her name sounded when he spoke it, maybe even better than when he called her sunflower names.

"I'll get my sweater." She felt a rush of blood to her face, a moment of dizziness. She scolded, *you are not a schoolgirl, Emma Green. Don't be silly.*

None-the-less, she felt a skip of delight in her step when Howard took her elbow. The morning sun danced through the garden, highlighting the enormous variety of color. They walked slowly. Emma listened to the shuffle of their side-by-side steps, punctuated by the regular tap of Howard's cane.

The head of her mammoth sunflower was tipped low, shyly wakening, its yellow petals dwarfed by the enormity of its center. She was thankful for the special attention she had given it. Its stalk was strong and could still support the enormous weight of its growing seeds. By mid-day, it would be standing proud and tall.

A tune in the form of a hum burst from Emma's chest as they passed the sunflower. She couldn't help herself. She'd always had a melody for her sunflowers. Howard squeezed her elbow and when she looked at him, he was smiling.

"You are my sunshine…" His voice started in, low and raspy. "…my only sunshine…" It reminded her of the way Edward used to sing, more of a speak-along, but with the proper rhythm. She allowed her own voice to join his. "… you make me happy, when skies are gray…"

They studied blooms on opposite sides of the sidewalk as the last line came to their lips. "… You'll never know, Dear, how much I love you…" Emma straightened her arm, feeling Howard's fingers release at her elbow. She found them with her own, and they held hands as they finished the song, loudly and together. "…please don't take… my sunshine… away…"

Howard didn't seem to mind Emma's attention to the mammoth sunflower. At first, when they met for breakfast in the garden, she'd slip her bits of cereal to the plant when she thought Howard wasn't looking. But soon she was back to her old ways, feeding the flower first, even talking to it as casually as she had talked to Howard. He never said a word about it, never once acted surprised or questioned her sanity. She appreciated this, just as she appreciated the stories he told about his daughter and son who lived on opposite coasts, both far from the center of everything in Kansas.

She didn't even mind, in fact, looked forward to, the news about Howard's grandkids. He had five—two boys from his daughter, one just starting college, the other near the end of high school, and three girls from his son. There was Mara, Howard's favorite, who had just turned eleven and was an accomplished piano player just as Howard's wife had been, and Kelsey and Hannah, the twins, only three years old and somehow always finding trouble to get into.

Emma smiled. Howard was relating the tale of the twins' latest escapade. She looked at the photos he was holding out to her across their coffee cups, delighted that she immediately recognized which twin was Kelsey, by the slight wave to her golden hair, and which twin was Hannah. Her hair hung straight like copper wire.

"They'll be coming," Howard was saying.

"Coming where? Who?" Emma righted herself. She hated feeling she had missed part of the conversation. She had been too engrossed in the photos and lost track of what Howard was talking about.

"The twins. Mara. They'll be visiting in August."

"Coming here?" Emma felt her heart sink. She'd grown used to Howard's attention. Now he was going to have family of his own visit. Grandkids. Maybe they would talk him into leaving. He was always telling her how his son wanted him to move to California. He had even described the retirement community his son had taken him to see. It was near a beach.

"Beautiful," Howard had pronounced it. "Imagine summer-time all year round."

Emma couldn't imagine living anywhere without proper seasons, though the winters were harder for her than they used to be. Her joints would grow stiff in the cold and she felt her walk was reduced to a shuffle when the snows covered the ground. She would huddle beneath her blankets and sip hot tea while listening to book tapes from the library. Reading was more difficult than it used to be, as well. Too many pages would give her a fit of headaches. It was frustrating, but determined to find a way around it, she had discovered this sound alternative to large print books. She would close her eyes and listen, falling into the stories much as she had in her youth… becoming, temporarily, someone in a story that could not possibly be her own.

"So what do you think?"

Emma's attention, again, was brought back around to Howard. She scowled, covering her frustration over having allowed herself to be so easily distracted.

"No? But you'll still join us, won't you?"

Howard seemed crestfallen. Not entirely sure of what she had just refused, Emma made a conscious decision to bite her tongue and carefully consider her response.

"I'm sorry," she finally said. "I was… mind wandering. That's all."

"So you will join us?" Howard looked at her with hope in his eyes.

The grandchildren. The conversation returned to Emma. *He was talking about the grandchildren visiting, and he is asking me to be a part of it.*

"Of course," she blurted with much more enthusiasm than she intended. She still didn't know where they were going, but he had invited her along. She tapped her toes a couple of times on the concrete beneath to release her joy.

"And you're sure you won't change your mind about entering the sunflower? It's sure to be a winner. I've never seen one so big."

Pride broadened the smile on Emma's face. "Of course," she said again, feeling inexplicably ready to agree to just about anything.

Howard was right. Mara was a beautiful, expressive young lady. She spoke with the eloquence of an adult, yet her eyes widened at the turn of every corner, as delighted by the sights of the county fair as her younger sisters, who were going to be celebrating their fourth birthdays while in town with their Grandpa Howard. Emma had already received an invitation and was nearly bubbling with anticipation. She hadn't been to a child's birthday party in years, decades maybe.

They passed through the vegetables, eyes marveling at the displays of squash, green beans, potatoes, and mouths watering over the perfect red ripeness of so many tomatoes. Emma felt that everyone was as eager to reach the flower displays as she was. Howard had talked her into entering, not only her largest sunflower, but an assortment of other blooms, as well.

Howard directed his son and daughter-in-law to the first long row of marigolds. He flipped the card on the bright orange marigold, the most obvious winner, with a big purple ribbon attached. "Emma Green!" Howard's son read the card aloud and winked at her.

Purple and blue ribbons, every one of them. Emma tried to shame herself for being so prideful, but it wasn't working. She felt herself standing taller and the smile wouldn't leave her face.

Sunflower heads lined the back wall of the building. For a moment, Emma felt a bit of remorse seeing her beauty uprooted and leaning on its marvelous thick stalk against the wall. But it was dying anyway, she reminded herself. And here, beside so many puny mammoths, her sunflower stood high above the crowd, its diameter dwarfing its rivals. Two frilled ribbons, twice the size of the other fair ribbons, were fastened to its head. A poster on the wall read, "1st Prize - Largest Sunflower - Emma Green" and beneath that, "1st Prize - Prettiest Sunflower - Emma Green."

They gazed upon the sunflowers; even the twins quieted for a moment. Mara moved closer, and Emma accepted the smooth, warm hand as the girl laced her fingers through Emma's own. She smiled down at the lovely girl, so close to entering the season of her bloom.

"Will you teach me?" the girl said solemnly. "Teach me to grow flowers the way you do?"

"Of course," Emma responded with a voice soft and entirely appropriate. She felt Howard watching her, and she knew he was smiling. She squeezed the girl's smooth hand and gazed upon her sunflower.

A cluster of white-haired women was gathering in front of the sunflower display. Still holding Mara's hand, Emma turned to go.

"Emma!" a voice rang out. "Emma Green!"

She turned back to find Iris Finnegan waving wildly. The old woman pushed from the cluster and rushed forward at a speed Emma had not thought Iris capable. She grabbed Emma's free hand and petted her like a small critter.

"Ladies," Iris called the white-hairs to attention. "This is Emma Green. We can all thank Emma for the beauty that fills our gardens at Sunnyside Acres."

The ladies cooed and greeted Emma enthusiastically. "What a beauty," one gestured to the highest sunflower on the wall. "Absolutely marvelous," another said. "I could use some tips," another exclaimed. "You obviously have a way with flowers."

Emma was too embarrassed to mumble more than a few words of thanks, clinging to Mara's hand like a lifeboat in uncharted waters. Mara led her back toward Howard's family.

"Oh Emma," Iris's voice floated to them over the noise of the crowd. "Perhaps you'll join us for tea later this week."

Emma looked down at Mara who was smiling up at her. "Of course," she said, surprising herself. It even came out in an entirely soft and civil manner. "Tea in the garden, before the season is over," Emma said. "That would be glorious."

She could see Howard and Iris, both nodding their heads in agreement.

Meg folded her legs yogi style and dropped in the center of the dusty gravel road. "Man, you can see everything from here," she said.

"Everything... which is nothing," Shannon answered with a sigh. "I hate this town."

"Not everything," wheezed Jimmy, still making his way up the hill. "You can see a lot, but you can *not* see the future from here."

"That's stupid, Jimmy," Shannon said. "Of course you can't see the future. It's not a place. It's just time we haven't gotten to yet."

"Maybe if you two can start being nice to each other, we will all still be friends when the future arrives," Meg said.

"Shh... I hear something," Shannon said.

Jimmy dropped to his knees beside the girls, then scooted forward and squinted, looking toward the wild sunflowers and weeds that invaded the road at the bottom of the hill. "I think it's her. It's the witch," he whispered.

"Stop calling her that," said Meg. "Just because she's old and lives alone, that doesn't make her a witch."

"She talks to cats," Shannon said. "And they listen."

"It's true," Jimmy said. "Stevie said Bethany said that her cousin Frank's girlfriend saw the witch when the moon was full and *all* the cats from Birch Fall were around her in a circle."

The kids watched and waited.

Jimmy huffed and wheezed.

"Sit downwind," Shannon commanded. "You stink, Jimmy. Go over there."

"Would you at least try to be nice to him?" Meg pleaded. "Jimmy can't help that he's heavy."

Shannon shook her head, got up, and moved to the other side of the road. "He has always been perfectly happy by himself. Every summer he has spent alone in his big old house with his creepy uncle. I don't know why you have to drag him out, make him come with us."

"He's my cousin," Meg said. "Family is important, and if you don't like my family, Shannon, then you don't need to like me either."

Jimmy turned his back to Shannon and put his elbows on his knees. He watched his cousin, Meg. "Thanks for dragging me," he said. "It's kind of boring at my house. I like hanging out with you better than being alone…"

Jimmy's voice rose, "and I like hanging out with Shannon, even though she hates me."

Behind the kids, the Birch Fall courthouse and town center, bordered on the north end by the river, sat like a storybook diorama beneath an impossibly blue Kansas sky. In front of them, the crunchy gravel road fell into wild disrepair and dropped steeply into a mess of unkempt trees that mostly hid the old house where the newest resident of Birch Fall lived.

Only a crooked chimney—minus a few bricks—was visible through the leafy green foliage, but the girls knew the house well. The front door had been secured by a two-by-four and a padlock. There was a window on the back porch that could be slid open from the outside. Meg and Shannon, and a near-dozen Birch Fall kids who would enter junior high in the fall, had played in the house frequently after school. Pretty much every kid except Jimmy, who rarely ventured far from the comfort of his own home, considered the old house public property.

Meg's father had expressed surprise when he heard someone had purchased the house and moved into it. "It can't possibly be safe," Meg overheard her father tell her mother. "Does the house have electricity? Running water?"

"I don't know about you, but I ain't riding my bike down that hill," Jimmy said, looking toward the steep drop-off and then back to the gradual, but long incline from which they had come. "Cause if I ride down that side, I have to come up again, and I ain't riding up again."

"Why are we here?" asked Shannon. "My mom already sent the welcome wagon. She took a pie from the diner the day the lady moved in."

"So your mom's seen her? She's met the witch?" Jimmy's eyes grew big and a smile split his round face.

Shannon shook her head. "No, she said nobody answered the door. She left it there in a cooler with a note."

The sound of rusty door hinges echoed through the trees below. Meg bit her lip. Shannon shielded her eyes from the glare of the sun. They both stared and waited for the old woman to wander far enough from the house to be seen. It wasn't a woman that came into view, however. It was an upside down boy.

"Who's that? What's he doing?" Shannon whispered.

"He's walking on his hands." Meg shrugged, as if it were the most natural thing in the world for a boy to do.

The boy flipped gracefully to his feet and dusted his hands on his jeans as he stood upright. He walked, feet down, through the tall weeds that bordered the road. He disappeared into the trees, and when he reappeared, he carried three short sticks, tossing one and then another into the air. When he reached the middle of the road, he stopped and faced the trio perched at the top of the hill. The boy bowed deeply and began to juggle.

"He sees us!" Shannon whispered.

Meg's eyes were bright, her whole face shining. "Of course he sees us. We're right here. Let's go introduce ourselves."

By the time the girls reached the bottom of the hill, the upside down boy, still right side up, was juggling sticks so quickly it was hard to see where one ended and the next began. He reached behind his back and caught one, then beneath his leg for another. He juggled while giving the girls the impression he only had eyes for them.

"Come one, come all," he said when they were close enough to see that his eyes matched the color of the sky. "See the boy wonder. The amazing Tully. There is no other as skilled. As talented. As dexterous. As daring."

With that, the boy threw the sticks extra high, one after the other, and cleanly did a back flip before catching them again.

"You forgot to mention humble," Meg said. "I'm Meg Elkin, and this is Shannon Ost."

"There is no room for humility in the circus," the boy answered, grasping all three sticks with one hand and bowing again. "Tully Sorey, at your service."

"You're in the circus?" Shannon asked.

The boy shrugged. "Was. Until my mother decided we needed to settle down and find a place to call home. I think she's trying to civilize me before it's too late."

"Your mother thinks Birch Fall is civilized?" Shannon said. "She knows, like, 280 people live here, right?"

The girls looked at each other and giggled.

"Hey," Jimmy shouted, only having made it about half way down the hill. "Where'd you learn to do that?"

Shannon sighed. Meg turned and watched as her cousin stumbled toward them. By the time he reached the girls and the juggling boy, his face was beet red with sweat dripping from his forehead. Shannon cringed when Meg reached out a hand to steady her cousin.

"That was really cool," Jimmy said. "Can you teach me? Not the walking on your hands. I could never do that. But the juggling? Do you think you could teach me how? I'm good with a yo-yo. I bet I could juggle."

"Tully Sorey," Meg said. "This is my cousin, Jimmy Grimes."

Tully nodded and extended a hand. Jimmy didn't respond until Meg took him by the elbow and pushed his whole arm toward Tully's, encouraging a shake.

"Jimmy, this is Tully Sorey," she said. "He is a former circus boy and our newest neighbor."

"We don't ever get new people 'round here," Jimmy said, letting go of Tully's hand and pulling his t-shirt up to wipe at his face.

Tully's eyebrows rose as Jimmy exposed his soft, white belly.

"Very nice to meet you Jimmy Grimes. I would be more than happy to teach you to juggle," the circus boy said.

"Wow," Jimmy said, looking from Meg to Tully, his face shining with a dozen kinds of happy. "That would be cool. Really cool. I'm a good student. I learn fast."

Meg smiled at Tully and winked.

"What circus were you in?" Shannon asked, crossing her arms tight across her chest. "I've been to the Barnum and Bailey in Topeka, and I never saw you."

"It was more of like, a side show," Tully answered with a shrug. "Bearded ladies, two headed snakes, the world's smallest man, conjoined twins…"

"Like at the state fair?" Meg asked.

Tully shrugged again. "Sure, we did some state fairs, but never in Kansas."

"Freak show," Jimmy said.

"Yeah," Tully answered, "a lot of freaks, and me, Tully the Boy Wonder."

"Because you walked on your hands?" Meg said.

"Acrobatics. Juggling. I was a staple act, central to the show."

"What did your mom do?" Shannon asked.

"Bearded lady!" Jimmy shouted before cracking up with laughter. "Or… or… or…." He bent over, trying to catch his breath. "The fat lady. The ginormous one who sings. Was that your mom?"

Meg furrowed her brow and put a firm hand on Jimmy's shoulder. "That's not nice," she said, shaking her head. "Be nice, Jimmy."

"It's fine," Tully said watching warily as Jimmy's whole body shook with silent laughter. "My mother is a fortune teller. Crystal balls, palm reading, tarot cards, stuff like that."

Jimmy sobered quickly. He stood upright, the smile completely fading from his face. "For reals?" he said softly. "Your mom really is a witch? Do you believe in that stuff? Can your mom see the future?"

Shannon ran her hands over her arms, suppressing a shiver. "There's no such thing," she said flatly. "That stuff is all made up. Nobody knows the future. It's just an act like everything else in a circus… or a freak show, whatever you're from."

Tully crossed his arms and looked at Shannon, the brow above his pale blue eyes creasing until the girl was forced to look away. "Is it?" he asked. "Are you saying you don't believe?"

The boy looked toward the old house hidden in the trees.

"I bet I can predict something about your future," Tully said, turning back around slowly, challenging Shannon with a cold blue stare.

"Like it would matter," Shannon answered, but the boy had already pulled a round stone out of his pocket. It looked like a clear marble, but was much larger. He was holding it, palm up, balanced on his fingers, peering through it at the girl who frowned at him.

Tully began to walk around her.

"A crystal ball? Really?" Shannon said.

"Cool," Jimmy said. "Do me next. Look at me through that thing."

"It's not actually a gazing ball," Tully said. "But I've been known to get impressions. Just glances of the future, now and then."

He continued walking in a circle, one eye squinted nearly closed as he watched the clear stone balanced on his hand. When he stopped, he gripped the ball in his fist and shook his head. "Not much here," he said. "I mean, clearly you have a future. It's all clean and bright and shiny. You're a good girl. You'll do alright. But there's nothing remarkable there. Nothing really interesting. In other words, you don't have a whole lot to look forward to."

"Ha, ha," Jimmy yelled. "There's nothing remarkable about you, Shannon Ost. Nothing to look forward to."

Meg stood to the side, clearly on the edge of scolding her friends again, but Tully lifted the stone in her direction and said after only a moment, "Now you, Meg Elkin, are a different story. I don't need the assistance of magic to see that."

Tully walked a circle around Meg, holding the crystal between them. He nodded his head, tilted it to one side, as if listening to a voice from afar. When he finally stopped after two full circles, he looked pensive.

"Well?" Shannon said. "What did the Great and Marvelous Tully learn about Meg's future?"

"That she'll be great and marvelous," the boy said quietly, dropping his gaze to the ground.

"Me! Me!" Jimmy shouted.

"Jimmy, you don't have to yell," Meg said.

"Please," Jimmy whispered loudly. "Look at me through your crystal ball, Tully. Tell me my future." Jimmy closed his eyes and jumped up and down, excitement rippling through his whole body.

Tully looked from Meg, to Jimmy, and back again. "Sure," he said. "I guess."

The boy lifted the palm of his hand. His fingers visibly shook. He paused for a moment, trying to get the stone to balance on his fingers as he had before. He finally settled for grasping the crystal between his thumb and his index finger. He held it out like a magnifying glass, closed one eye, and peered in Jimmy's direction. Tully started walking around the pudgy boy who stood still grinning and squeezing his eyes tight in anticipation.

A stream of sunlight seemed to streak through the stone suddenly, striking Jimmy's chest with a pattern of light.

Meg gasped, and Shannon jumped.

Tully dropped the crystal and stumbled backward.

When Jimmy stepped forward to help the circus boy to his feet, Tully was shaking his head. "No," he said quietly. "I must have saw it wrong."

"Who you talking to?" Jimmy asked. "What'd you see? What about my future?"

"Nothing," Tully said. "It's… not a good day for it. I can't see anything. I don't really know the future. It's just an act. It's a performance, like she said."

Without another word, Tully turned, pushed his way through the shallow ditch, high with weeds, and disappeared.

Meg, Shannon, and Jimmy waited, looking to one another.

Meg bent and picked up the crystal Tully had dropped. She lifted it and looked toward Shannon, then Jimmy, pausing and staring at her cousin through the crystal ball for a long time. She finally dropped the large marble-like object into the front pocket of her blouse.

"I think he's lying," Meg said. "That boy? Tully? He knows things. I think he saw the future."

A Life in Progress

for Melissa McLoughlin

There are mornings when I stand in front of the mirror too long, hoping to catch a glimpse of myself. The self I am inside my head. The self I expect to see before the mirror shows me reality.

It is not that I still think of myself as nineteen. I have no desire to be that young, that anxious and unfocused, again. It is not even my mother I see in my place anymore. This woman in front of me is starting to look an awful lot like my grandmother. She scrutinizes every laugh line. She uses the back of her hand to press the wattle that seems to be forming beneath her chin. I can see through her thinning skin, a blue network of veins at her temple. They also decorate the backs of her hands alongside browned age-spots. This woman's hair is streaked with silver, looking nothing like my own deep, dark black.

The mirror is smudged by traces of my own fingertips. How many times have I reached out to touch her, trying to reconcile the fact that she, this woman growing older, is me?

I was well into my thirties before I made up my mind that I was a strong, independent woman. How is it that my brain has failed to update this image? Why is the woman I expect to see, morning after morning, so smooth skinned, without my depth of experience around the eyes?

Perhaps it is a sign of age that I can't seem to remember how much I've changed. My face, almost forty years older than I imagine it must look, has surprised me again.

"Chelle?" Babs calls. "Are you ready to go?" She walks into my bedroom as if she owns the place. And why wouldn't she? We've been friends for forty years now, roommates for nearly twenty. She is the sister I never had, the twin of my heart, the finisher of my sentences, the one who helps me find answers to questions I still can't articulate. We know each other's truths, and I imagine my heart would be cleaved in half if she were ever to leave me.

She places a warm hand on my arm and leans her head against my shoulder, sharing my space in the mirror for a moment. We stare at our reflections. Babs masks her age with hair color, but it doesn't stop two old women from staring back at us.

"We're going to be late," she whispers, and I think she must feel the wonder of it too, the mystery of our own aging, the reluctance of our brains to update the mental images of ourselves.

As I turn away, I catch the glimpse I was longing for. Just out of the corner of my eye, I see her. She may not be young, but she's still familiar, strong, and vibrant. I square my shoulders. Babs looks back at me and smiles.

Babs and I ride together to town in comfortable silence as we've done every day for years. I drop her off in the circle drive in front of the administration building of the university. She handles student loans, gifts, and grants, all manner of numbers that hold no interest for me. Her co-workers have started asking her if she has plans to retire. She tells me that she dreams about it, but she's not sure what she would do with herself. She enjoys life at the university, surrounded by so many youngsters still looking forward to their prime.

After dropping Babs off, I drive the ten blocks across town to the office of Heiggens and Grant, an old-school advertising and print agency grown modern. It's a good-sized business for our small town, with more than twenty full-time employees and a dozen more who work part-time or flexible shifts from home. We have specialists in everything from film and video to online retail database management, web hosting, and print and digital graphic design.

Forty years ago I proudly called myself an artist, but had no idea how to turn my art into a career that paid the bills. My skills at hand-lettering landed me a job with Heiggens Media. I slowly gained confidence and ended up dragging the company into the digital age after a fling with a computer geek—they were new and interesting back then—who introduced me to a tablet input device and computer software for illustrators. I was so enamored I gave up eating out for a year and took out a personal loan for $6,000 to purchase my own, state-of-the-art computer for the office. Within three years, Edward Heiggens offered me second billing on the sign out front, and I pretty much took over the creative direction of the company from there.

I somewhat retired a few years ago, but I still go in to work each day and continue to draw and illustrate to my heart's content. What I have given up is the management of others. I've put aside the ceaseless pursuit of staying on top of the latest and greatest in graphics technology. I advise when necessary, but have handed the reins of the company to Allison Blaufass, an amazingly talented young woman who leaves me green with envy if I'm not careful with my thoughts.

It's not exactly that she reminds me of myself at her age. She's got drive and focus where I kind of stumbled onto something that just happened to work for the company. I am content thinking of her as the daughter I never had.

"Good morning, Chelle," Allison calls as I enter, "I'm going to need you to give a tour and spend some time with one of the new hires this morning."

I inwardly sigh, but smile as Allison catches my eye. "Anything you need," I say reflexively. Last week I was approached by a local author to illustrate a children's book. I haven't been this excited about getting started on a project in years, but I've also been encouraging Allison to use me if and when she needs me. Babs recently suggested that I might come off as a bit intimidating, and while I am very happy to have Allison in charge of the day-to-day business, I don't want her to struggle because she's uncomfortable asking for my assistance.

Mae White is sitting at her desk sorting papers as Allison looks over her shoulder. Mae is the only employee who has been with the company longer than I have. That is, if you don't count Ed, which most of us no longer do. He's as physically slow as he is senile. Last year, Mae refurbished his office with a bunch of blue-lined paste-ups she found in storage, and Ed is still happily designing ads with exacto knives and colored pencils, just as he did when Heiggens Media began. Allison, bless her heart, throws him real assignments once in a while and several times has incorporated his renderings into the final product.

I, on the other hand, steer clear of Ed more than I care to admit. Worse than my mirror, Ed reminds me that we are closer to the end of things than the beginning. Fifteen years my senior, he's been everything to me in the course of forty years, from boss and mentor, to lover and friend. I spent years being thankful that we'd somehow managed to avoid breaking up his marriage. Mrs. Heiggens was always kind and tolerated me. I somehow imagined that she knew what we tried to hide. My guilt was enough to push me to marry the company itself, to give Ed more time to be a good family man. I made up for the low points of my life by propelling Heiggens and Grant to such economic proportions that Mrs. Heiggens and her children never had to want for anything.

Mrs. Heiggens passed away three years ago, and Ed's mental health took a significant dive.

"The new guy's name is Jeremy," Mae says. "He's waiting in your office."

Mae is looking over the tops of her glasses, waiting for me to gather my professional wit and roll with it. Allison doesn't seem to want to make eye contact with me, so I respond a little too brightly. "Sure!" I say. "I'd love to."

I'm barely two steps down the hall when I hear the sound of Ed's voice singing, "Me-Chelle, my Belle." The tones are deep and clear and even. I turn to look at Allison and Mae, who both respond by widening their eyes at me and then turning back to the task at Mae's desk.

Ed appears in the hallway before me and my gut immediately fills with that same, flip-floppy travelling-through-time sensation, much like the one experienced during this morning's mirror encounter. Who is this old man standing in front of me? He sounds so much like my old lover, my friend.

The present rushes over me, and I remind myself that those feelings, those people, were long ago. The old man smiles, but it is a younger Ed's smile, the seductive one that once reeled me in when

I was young and soft and impressionable, though Ed always claimed that it was I who had hooked him. Either way, we'd gotten over it. We'd recovered gracefully and gone on to run a successful business, first me as Ed's underling and then as his equal. Now, I suppose I qualify as his caretaker, though I've done everything in my power to avoid taking an active role in his day-to-day activity. It's Mae who answers his children's calls. Mae makes sure he has "work" to do, even when she's re-running old files from businesses that no longer exist. She keeps him busy, happy, and as engaged as he is able.

I touch my fingers to my forehead, suppressing the desire to close my eyes and turn away from him. God willing, I'll never have to play a role in changing this man's diaper. It occurs to me that I could use a few lessons in growing old gracefully.

Ed is still smiling. His eyes are clear, the color of milk chocolate topped with flecks of gold. I wonder if his head is clear, as well, this morning. He continues to hum our old song, and I fear this means his mind is wandering somewhere in the past. He's got a bandage on his nose. I remember Mae telling me that they removed skin cancer last week.

"Good morning, Ed," I say. "Lovely day."

"We should go to Florida," he says. "We could buy one of those RV's. We could travel. See the world."

"Together? You and me, Ed?"

"Sure. Why not? We were always good together. Just look at this place. It's proof we could do something right, no? Heiggens and Grant. It may just outlive both of us."

I try to see through him, to the internal workings of his mind. Years ago we'd stopped referring to our tryst. We buried it, ignored it until it was so stale neither of us thought of it on a daily basis. Was he now acknowledging it, or was he there again, in the past? Or was he simply referring to our success as business partners, honestly suggesting that we might move into the twilight of our lives together?

"What are we still doing here, anyway?" he says. The smile has dropped from his face. "I'm drawing pictures like a child. Not real work. I haven't done any real work in years. Not since Angela died. What are we still doing here?"

I feel a lump rise in my throat and do my best to swallow it, though my eyes betray me and threaten to fill with tears. I remember Jeremy, and the fact that he's probably sitting in my office listening to every word that is spoken between Ed and I.

"Well, Ed, I'm illustrating a book," I say. I pull the sketchpad from my bag, flip open the cover, and turn it so that he can see the penciled drafts.

Ed nods his head. His eyes search mine, and for a moment I find myself wishing my mind were more like his, perhaps fuzzy about the details, perhaps believing that today is actually yesterday, and that all I know about the truth of time from my morning glance in the mirror is already gone.

"I forget you're still so young," he says softly. "That's nice, your illustrations. And exciting, a book. We should have done more of that type of thing around here."

I step around him, conscious that I am trying to appear relaxed, settled, and content with the way things are. If only he didn't look so old. If only we still had years and years ahead of us, molding and shaping the business, thinking more about the direction we are headed rather than about where we have been.

"I think I should move," he says, following me. "There are some nice apartments up by the kids. My son wants me to look at them. Retirement places. Homes for old folks like me. They'd send in help for my bad days. Cooking. Cleaning. Then if things go way south…"

He stops here. I don't know if he wants me to argue with him, or agree. I give a sort of half-shake, half-nod of my head, leaving it to him to interpret it as he pleases. Selfishly, I think about how much easier it would be not to have to see him each day. This person I am becoming inside my head—I do not like her.

This seems like a conversation I should have with Ed. He is my oldest friend. We had years of working well together after the mistakes of our early time together, before his wife died and his mind began to grow noticeably cloudy. He seems as clear-headed as I have seen him in a long, long time, but how would I know, the way I avoid him at every turn. When was the last time I met my friend Ed, face-to-face?

"I know, Ed," I say, but what I know, I cannot tell him. I try again. "We should talk about this." I know I don't mean it, but it somehow feels better having said it. "After lunch?" I hear myself ask. "Maybe this evening? We could grab a bite."

"Paul is coming," he says. "My boy. He's picking me up this afternoon. He's taking me to try out the new place."

Mae is coming down the hall behind Ed. She's nodding, affirming for me that what Ed says is true. She looks sad, perhaps she feels a little bad that she had not told me sooner. But I'm just projecting, I realize. It is I who feels bad that I have let Ed fade away like this, that I've removed myself so completely from his life, though we are in the same office every day, that I have not even been made part of this new plan. Ed is moving away. Ed, inevitably, will get older, even more forgetful, and will eventually die. What will remain of Heiggens and Grant when a Heiggens is no longer here?

"Jeremy Davis," Mae is standing at the doorway to my office, ushering me past Ed. Perhaps she sees that I need rescued. Perhaps she's simply being kind to poor Jeremy, who has been sitting, waiting, for his first day at Heiggens and Grant to begin.

"Jeremy Davis," she repeats. "Allow me to introduce you to Chelle Grant. She'll be your tour guide for the morning. She'll be answering all of your questions about our little company."

Before I head into the office, I put my arms around Ed. He's thin, much frailer than I think he should be. I can feel the tremor in his palsied hands as he pats me on the back.

More than an hour later, I am still in my office, sitting across the table from Jeremy, the new guy. He's handsome to the core. Dark curly hair and the kind of long lashes that every woman envies. His eyes are the color of coffee beans. His skin is creamy mocha. I find myself wanting to reach out, to lift him to my lips, to drink him up.

I tip my head back and laugh at something he says, and then remind myself what I must look like to him. As much as this feels like flirting, I simply can't allow it. I'm at least a decade past cougar. If I had children, he would be my grandchild.

I am delighted, however, to learn that I hold the power to surprise him. He doesn't expect someone like me, someone my age, to be knowledgeable about computers, and certainly not graphics software, never mind to show any amount of competency in design and editing on his level.

He is immediately sucked into my catalog of illustrations. I've been doing this for forty years. My digital portfolio began before his birth. My palette is immense compared to this young man's dabbling.

Physically, he closes the gap between us as I tell him stories about the old days in computerized illustrating. I show off, throwing in notes about my travels and speaking engagements. It's not that I want to impress him; I want him to see me as an equal. It's obvious that our skills, our interests lie in similar playing fields. It's the years between us that make this flutter against my ribcage awkward. I feel the heat that radiates from his body, sitting so close to mine. I inhale his scent and close my eyes and remind myself that I am waning. He has only just begun.

Telling Jeremy about Heiggens and Grant is immensely pleasurable. I fill him in on our history. He hangs on my every word, and I find it delicious. I feel young and full of light, and I refuse to glance in the mirror when I take a bathroom break before lunch. I won't risk anything mellowing my high.

Mae orders sandwiches for us to eat in my office, and I tell Jeremy stories about my first trip to London. The subject of world travel lights up his face, so I tell him about Paris, Italy, Greece, and even the two weeks in Brazil with the mysterious Paulo whom I met on a plane and briefly thought I might love.

It's well after lunch before we start the official tour of the office. We meet Paul and Ed in the hallway. Ed's boy hugs me politely. He's barely a decade my junior, and was the only one of Ed's children who ever knew, who understood that I had loved his father for a time. I suppose, at one time, Paul hated me, but it didn't show now.

The encounter leaves me feeling as disoriented as I imagine Ed must feel much of the time. I was young again, only moments ago, sitting at that table and reliving the past in storied form. Yet here is Ed's son, older than Ed had been when we were lovers, and Ed, an age beyond recognition even when I am acknowledging my own. I make hasty promises in the hallway. I tell Ed I will visit. I wish him luck with his move, which sounds so odd and miscalculated once I have said it, but I have no way of reeling it back in and exchanging it with more appropriate words.

I remember to introduce Jeremy at the last minute and then drag him down the hallway to where the younger generation of Heiggens and Grant employees prefer to station themselves. The large, common-room has taken the place of the individual office spaces I once thought of as a luxury. Allison knocked out nearly all the walls, aside from mine and Ed's, when I gave her the reins of the company. I watch Jeremy's eyes light up when a younger employee explains to him that he can basically claim any empty space in the room that he desires, and that he can cobble together a work station from the tables, desks and chairs in storage or build himself something from scratch in the shop on the back of the property if he wishes.

By the time we have made our way to the video and production rooms in the basement, I have managed to push Ed far from the front of my mind and am focusing on the new hire, once again. In fact, I enjoy my day with Jeremy so much that I forget all about my sketches and plans for the book. Words continue to tumble out of my mouth as my mind filter has long decided it is useless to attempt to interfere. Before I know it, I've invited Jeremy to join me at How-Dee's Bar after office hours.

He accepts without hesitation.

We walk the four blocks from the office to the bar and I text Babs that I've made plans with coworkers. She sends a message back that she's going to eat at the Chinese restaurant near the university and will then read by the central fountain until I choose to pick her up. I promise her I won't be late, and she returns a text noting that if her ex comes along, she'll ask him for a ride and will let me know if/when I've been relieved of shuttle service.

I lead Jeremy to my favorite table at How-Dee's and order us cheese fries and chicken wings. We drink beer and talk nonstop. As the evening wears on, the music gets louder and the lights grow dimmer. Jeremy has moved from sitting across the table to beside me, ostensibly so that he can better hear. It almost feels like a real connection until he looks into my eyes and wistfully says, "Man, I wish my grandma were as cool as you."

It's well after dark by the time I pull into the drive. Babs is sitting in a lawn chair in the garage, lit by a single bulb hanging from a wire in the center of the ceiling and laughing at something Carl has said. Carl is Babs's ex-husband. He's winterizing our lawn mower and drinking our cheap beer. They've had a better life together as a divorced couple for twenty years than most people ever manage through the prime years of wedded bliss. She left me once, early on, to go back to him. They didn't last the second time either, yet Carl has been our faithful lawn manager and handyman without hesitation.

When Carl leaves, Babs and I sit in the lawn chairs in the garage and watch the moon rise in the night sky. We play a game we call alternate lives.

"If you had married the first boy you ever kissed, where would you be now?" I ask.

She starts telling a story that includes mentally handicapped kids with buck teeth. When she was nine, it turns out, her cousin Gordon kissed her on a dare.

"If you had married Ed," she says, "instead of walking away when he was about to leave his family."

I shake my head. "Words cannot express how wrong that reality would be," I say quietly.

"Ok, try this one," she says, sensing that maybe steering clear of Ed would be a good thing. "If you could have your thirty-year-old body back, what would you be doing tonight?"

"What? Or whom?" I say, grinning wickedly in her direction.

Babs raises her eyebrows. "Do tell," she says.

"His name is Jeremy, and if I were 30, or at least in possession of my 30-year-old body again? Yep, I'd be all over him. He'd still be too young, but at 30 it wouldn't have mattered."

"Jeremy," Babs says. "New hire at the office?"

I nod and touch my finger to my nose.

"How about you?" I say.

Babs throws back her head and laughs, then quickly turns sober. "Probably Carl," she answers with a sigh. "Damn that man. He drives me crazy, but after all these years, he's still the one who heats my loins."

I feel her watching me. I know she's longing for a cigarette after thinking about sex with Carl. I have to admit, Carl and I have never been close, but he's as attractive to me now as he has ever been.

"Do you think men ever feel this way?" I ask. "Like they've turned a corner and there's no going back?"

"Going back where?" Babs scoffs. "To the good old days? Perky tits and a still-tight ass? Is that really what we've worked so hard for?"

"A little, yeah," I admit. "I mean, I feel like I was coasting for so long. An endless road of possibility before me."

"You're sixty-seven and in fantastic shape," Babs scolds. "Stop your belly-aching. You're still a life in progress, and you aren't going to convince me otherwise."

"Sixty-seven is a long way from fifty," I answer. "And it sure as hell isn't forty anymore."

Babs puts an arm around me and we let our heads fall together.

"Okay," she whispers. "So maybe it does suck a little, this getting old."

We hold hands and sit together until the moon has grown full and bright in the night sky. Memories pull at me until I am ten years old again, sitting with my best friend in the whole world, pondering the ways of the universe and wondering what it will feel like to finally be grown up.

"If you could be holding anybody's hand right now, watching this moon with anyone you wanted," Babs says.

I think of Jeremy and his creamy mocha skin. I think of Ed and the days of long ago when I thought I could actually love and make a life with the man. I think of Paulo and the other men who have drifted in and out of my life over the years.

"I think," I say, squeezing Babs's hand tight and pulling it close to press it against my heart. "I think I would choose to be right here with you, holding your hand, just like this."

Charade

I am not Annie Taylor.

And the woman sitting in this room in the tattered pink bathrobe with fuzzy blue slippers on her feet is not my mother.

"Annie!" the woman smiles at me. Her shriveled gray arms whip the air, beckoning.

"Hello, Aunt Vera," I say. My voice is barely a whisper.

I drop to my knees in front of the padded wooden rocker and accept this woman's hugs and kisses. She pets my hair and rubs my back. She launches into her sing-song babble, offering me after-school cookies and a glass of milk.

She reminds me to change into my everyday clothes before going outside to play.

I nod and smile, peeling myself from her grasp to perch on the edge of her bed.

Her eyes glow a brilliant blue.

"Do you know what today is, Annie?"

Annie's birthday.

"Your birthday, Annie. Your eighth birthday!" Aunt Vera giggles. Her eyes fill with tears, a mother who wishes her baby was not growing up so fast.

Annie's birthday. She would have been twenty-three this year. I am twenty-four.

My eyes wander over the cluttered walls of this little room. Baby Annie sleeping in pink pajamas. Toddler Annie with eyes and mouth wide open, holding a giant golden corncob. Annie and her favorite teddy bear. Annie's first day of school. Annie modeling a very grown-up, two-piece swimsuit. Aunt Vera braiding Annie's shining brown hair.

A lifetime disguises these drab, dirty white walls. Annie's lifetime.

Tucked behind the large, age-five portrait of Annie Taylor is the photograph I am seeking. It has yellowed, but not faded like the other photos on the wall.

I pull it from its hiding place and hand it to Aunt Vera.

She fingers it delicately. For a moment, her smile disappears and her brow wrinkles. The smile has returned by the time she looks to me.

"You and your cousin," she states simply.

"Annie — and — I," I say, and point to myself in the picture.

Two young girls, holding hands and beaming, have ice skates slung over their shoulders by the laces. I remember the chill in the air, but the sun was shining brightly. I am wearing a gray, hooded jacket, and Annie is wearing a beautiful, knitted, yellow sweater with red trim. It is a birthday present from her mother. It is adorned with eight knitted flowers, one red rose for each year of Annie's life.

Aunt Vera leans forward in her rocker until she has removed herself from it completely. She stands and begins her slow shuffle to the tiny, orderly closet. From within, she pulls a wide, flat box wrapped in girly pink paper.

The paper and bow are slightly different each year.

The content is the same.

I hold the box on my lap as Aunt Vera hovers over me. I slowly raise my head and look deep into her eyes.

"Aunt Vera," I say, "This isn't for me."

I perceive a flicker in her magnificent blue eyes. She appears to be holding her breath as she lowers herself slowly back into her rocking chair.

"Of course it's for you," she says.

For a moment, I wonder. Is this gift truly mine? A sweater, perhaps, knitted in my favorite color, blue. Perhaps not a sweater, but a set of Aunt Vera's famous winter accessories. I long to open the box and find a matching set: mittens, scarf, and cap.

"You two never should have gone skating on that pond." Aunt Vera startles me with the strength beneath her words. Her voice is deep. The delighted giggle is gone.

The ice was smooth. The temperature had dropped without wind, so there weren't even the usual frozen ripples that Annie and I delighted to skate upon. Aunt Vera had warned us to stay at the edge of the pond. She was following soon, to watch us. She trusted us to remain at the edge.

I peel the wrapping paper from the box, and I pause to look at Aunt Vera. She is staring past the photograph. Her face is solemn. Her blue eyes are empty, someone looking beyond time.

I know before I pull the lid all the way back that the beautiful yellow sweater with red trim is not my size. It is a sweater for a child, an eight-year old girl named Annie Taylor. I touch the knitted red roses, stitches identical to those I had admired on Annie's sweater so many years ago.

I pull the sweater to my face. The bulk absorbs my tears as I close my eyes and watch a young girl's face slip away into the deep, dark depths of a frozen farm pond. It's a vision, a memory of a wish I have seen time and time again. The young girl wears this yellow sweater, but the face is not Annie Taylor's.

It is my own.

Virtual Farm

"**K**evin is putting those buttons all over the barn now," Ed said, peering through the front window of the farmhouse that had been in his family for three generations. He watched as his son balanced on a thin sliver of a ladder. "If he's gonna go to all that trouble, he could take the time to grab a bucket and add some paint."

The buttons, as Ed referred to them, covered every outbuilding by now. Ramona applauded their son's efforts to find new and modern ways to make a living on the farm, but Ed couldn't see how fixing things up virtually did a bit of good for anybody.

"I let you coddle him too much," he mumbled.

Ramona glared.

"We never taught that boy to break a sweat. He never learned the value of a good hole dug. He never learned to take any pride in creating something from nothing with his hands."

"What do you call what he's doing right now?" Ramona answered, clearly angry.

"And what do we have to show for it?" Ed shot back. "A bunch of shiny buttons? He's probably making us a target for when the aliens land."

"Aliens schmaliens," Ramona said, snapping Ed on the backside with her kitchen towel. "I'm going to take the duct tape and attach those virtual glasses to your head permanently. Then we'll listen to you complain about your son's creative genius."

"Genius," Ed snorted. "We let him diddle on a computer till his brain went soft and now everyone thinks he's a genius."

Ed was taking off his shoes for bed when Kevin came in for the night. Ed listened as his son and wife discussed Kevin's project.

"It's ready?" Ramona asked. She sounded to Ed like a little girl.

Ed could hear them ripping open the box that had arrived via the brown delivery truck that morning. He'd seen dozens of pairs of his son's prototype glasses for the REGscape—Reality Enhancement Generation—project. His son wouldn't even take the time to try to explain it any longer, but Ed was no dummy. He wanted to appreciate that his son was thinking outside the box, but it was his job as a father to keep the boy grounded in reality. Kevin wasn't a child any longer. Gone were the days when they could simply affix their son's work to the refrigerator with magnets, letting him believe that any stick figure he drew was top-notch.

Kevin had settled on a design that looked something like a cross between scuba goggles and heavy duty sunglasses.

"You got 'em on right?" Kevin asked his mom. "Here, let me help you adjust them."

Ed sat on the edge of the bed, listening and waiting.

"Here it goes," Kevin said.

There was a period of silence before Ed heard his wife gasp. A note of wonderment escaped her, almost like she was warming up to sing. "Ahhhhh……"

Ed closed his eyes and shook his head. He got up and headed for the living room. Kevin and Ramona looked ridiculous in the REGscape goggles; heads tilted upward, mouths open.

"I'm standing in a castle," Ramona whispered. "It looks so real."

The inside of the house had been strewn with buttons for years, of course. It had started with the basement. Kevin had not even graduated from high school when his virtual house renovating had begun. Ed had almost grown accustomed to the shiny silver things, but staunchly refused to try on the specialized glasses his son claimed would liberate him from the dreary view that was their family's farm. Ed had come in one day from tilling the garden to find Ramona cooking while wearing an earlier version of the glasses she had on now. "Our son enhanced the kitchen," she laughed. "Martha Stewart would be so envious."

The only room inside the house that had not been strewn with buttons by now was Ed and Ramona's bedroom. He simply wouldn't allow it. He'd even threatened Kevin with expulsion from the house.

"And you are a knight in shining armor," Ramona said, looking at their son. She looked down. "And I must be a queen! Oh look at this gown. Isn't it lovely?"

She spun in a circle before noticing Ed was in the room. "Oh Ed. Isn't it lovely? The house is totally transformed. I can hardly believe it. I'm really standing here in my very own castle."

"You're standing in our living room wearing a dirty t-shirt," Ed answered.

Ramona wasn't fazed.

"Close your eyes, Mom. Wait for this one," Kevin's fingers tripped across a small keyboard.

"Oh my!" Ramona exclaimed, causing Ed to jump.

"What is it now?" he yelled. "Mount Saint Helens? Old Faithful? I suppose you're going to tell me we have a virtual Clint Eastwood serving milk and cookies before bed."

They ignored him and headed toward the door. Kevin held it open as Ramona stepped out onto the regular old farmhouse porch. The wood was rotting in several places. The railing had developed a significant lean to the north.

Ramona brought her hands up to her face. "Oh Kevin. It's beautiful. Absolutely perfect. The luminescent flowers, the forest floor, the butterflies."

Ed shook his head and turned away, escaping down the darkened hallway to the bedroom. Even with the door closed, he could hear Kevin explaining that the Enchanted Forest REGscape was going to be the setting for their first paid event. Chloe Nicholson, who had grown up down the road, was getting married and had reserved the farm for the occasion.

"I don't want people stomping through my garden," Ed yelled through the closed door. "I don't want..." he grumbled before punching his pillow and letting his body fall back on it.

Ed had given up dreams of making a living on the farm years earlier. He'd settled for safer work in the form of a weekly paycheck in the city. He drove forty-five minutes each way, five days a week, for nearly twenty-two years. They made extra income from the garden selling produce at the farmers' market. It wasn't perfect, but it was a purpose that had helped Ed maintain his sanity.

The plan had become one of sticking with the job in town through retirement. He and Ramona had talked about ways to grow their sales at the market. They'd talked of adding a roadside stand at the farm or perhaps starting a pick-your-own berry patch. When Ed was younger, all the rules were being written to run small guys out of business, but Kevin insisted tides were turning.

The job in town had let Ed go just last winter. Not quite three years till he would have been eligible for retirement. He heard they were serious about restructuring on a Monday and got notice that he was being laid off by quitting time on Wednesday.

"See you tomorrow," he'd said to his boss, with whom he thought he had a friendly relationship.

"Well actually, Ed..." the man had said as he handed him the envelope. "There've been some changes. It's nothing personal. We wish you luck."

There had been a pat on the shoulder and his boss was gone. He stuck the letter in his front pocket and drove all the way home to Ramona.

"I think I've been fired," he said, handing her the unopened letter.

"Fired?" she had asked, taking the envelope and slicing it open with the knife she'd been using to peel an apple.

Winter had never been so dark or so cold. Ed buried his disappointment in seed catalogs, aching for an early spring, spending every moment outdoors that he could manage. Kevin, on the other hand, had kept himself cloistered in the basement, coming up for meals only when Ramona insisted, and then only talking of this crazy plan to virtually enhance the farm as a setting for weddings and other events.

"I've got investors ready to go on this, Dad," Kevin said. "We open our farm to events this summer. Within a couple of years, we'll have REGscape installed on places across the country. This will surpass Community Shared Agriculture. It's the next big thing in agribusiness. Your farm doesn't need to be scenic, you've just got to have the wide open space to host people."

Ed watched mainly from his garden, the following week, as delivery trucks dropped off tables and chairs. In one afternoon, an enormous tent was raised beside the barn to serve as the station for the caterers. No matter how Ramona begged, Ed refused to put on the goggles to see the virtual wonder Kevin continued to program and tweak until well after dark each day in the week leading up to the neighbor girl's big event.

"You know you have to wear them on Chloe's wedding day," she scolded him. "If you don't, people will see you for exactly what you are."

"A lousy old farmer?" Ed countered.

Ramona clucked at him. "You must wear the goggles to become part of the REGscape. They mask you so that you'll fit in. You'll play your part."

"Like hell," Ed mumbled.

On the morning of the event, Kevin and Ramona were already out of the house by the time Ed got up. He pulled on his dress slacks and even put on a tie. It was a wedding, after all. He figured he ought to be respectful. When he got to the kitchen, a pair of goggles sat waiting for him in the middle of the table.

He sighed and tucked them under his arm. He stepped out onto the porch and marveled at the buzz of activity. Goggle-clad people were everywhere with smiles on their faces.

Ed reluctantly lifted the goggles and held them up to his face. It was as if the world immediately tilted. He felt a little dizzy. The rich and vibrant greens of the forest around him nearly pulsed. Small fairies flitted back and forth, their feet not even touching the ground. He pulled the goggles away and examined the people, real people, just like him. He lifted the goggles again, feeling his breath catch. Flitting fairies came into view.

No goggles; caterers carrying trays and stacks of white linens.

Goggles; fairies carrying intricately carved vessels and rainbow colored table coverings complete with garlands of exotic flowers.

"Mr. Anderson," a voice admonished him. "You know everyone signed an agreement that the goggles would remain on at all times."

He was speechless to see a beautiful woman with pointy ears and blue hair that seemed to writhe like snakes. She wore a shimmering gown that reminded him of soap bubbles. He pulled the goggles away from his face and recognized Neda Schuck, an acquaintance from church.

"Yes," Ed agreed. "I just..." he found his hands lifting the goggles to his face again. Neda was virtually stunning. He got a lump in his throat and lost all his words.

Ed pulled the strap of the goggles over the back of his head and settled them tightly against his face. He had to admit that the scenery took his breath away. It was a tremendous improvement over Kevin's early virtual remodeling of the basement only a few years before. It was a tremendous improvement over the faded old barn and yellowed grass pocked with dandelions.

Ed stepped carefully and found that he was able to navigate without any issue. He realized, with a jolt, that he was standing atop cloven hooves. He looked for a reflective surface. In a virtual babbling brook to the left he saw the very handsome head of a satyr looking back at him.

"I am a man-goat," he said, not knowing if he should feel pleased or recognize that this was his son's way of getting back at him for the lack of support.

He made his way through the busy fairies and forest creatures and breathed a sigh of relief when he recognized Ramona. She had goat ears of her own and wore a gauzy dress that flounced when she stepped. His image was to complement his wife's then. This knowledge relieved him.

"What's my job?" he barked, trying to hide any evidence of pleasure.

Ramona stepped close and kissed him on the cheek. Ed had expected not to feel it in the virtual state they were in, but the kiss felt entirely real.

"You're smiling," Ramona accused.

"Only virtually," Ed said.

He watched as Ramona's goat ears blurred and faded. For a moment she was entirely herself, and he realized she was lifting her goggles to look out beneath them.

"Oh no," she said. "That smile, Ed. It's entirely real."

Pages of Memory

"Nineteen eighty-seven," Ashley whispers as she passes me in the hall. Ashley is our night attendant. She replaced our last nurse, who was with us for three years, last spring.

"School going well?" I ask.

She nods and gives me a thumbs up sign. "I got in!"

"Of course you did," I say. "You're going to be one heck of a nurse practitioner."

I stop at the kitchen doorway to observe Maggie.

Her silver hair is swept up in a neat bun. She is wearing a scarlet blouse, and her head is bent over the table like she is studying something important. On some mornings Maggie sings to herself. Those are the mornings I can be fairly sure we are going to have a pleasant day. The only sound in the kitchen today is the hum of the refrigerator.

I clear my throat and make my way to the coffee pot. I pour a mug full, watching the steam curl up and around my fingers. When I turn, Maggie is staring at me.

"I suppose you are my husband," she says flatly.

"Twenty-seven years, my love," I answer.

"You're him?" She gestures to the pages on the table before her. "You're the man who questioned my priorities as a wife and mother?"

The year nineteen eighty-seven had been a very bad year for us.

"This is my handwriting. It says here that I am thinking of leaving you." She turns the page. I watch her eyes, deep pools of liquid blue, scan quickly. "Here. Two days later, I am still leaving you."

I breathe deeply, the smell of the coffee tickling my senses, giving me strength to have this conversation again. Why she so often selects this year from all the journals on the shelf, I can't imagine. I've tried removing it altogether, but she always notices its absence and that conversation is even worse than this one.

"I apologized," I say. "We worked it out."

Maggie won't let it go at that. This is the fiercely independent Maggie. It is this woman I fell in love with, the one who dazzled me with her intelligence and left me star-struck and love-sick in a way that deeply offended even my own mother. It was this Maggie; yet it wasn't. The woman sitting in front of me now has lost her sense of humor. Her blue eyes are missing that sparkle that appeared when she would pull my leg, egg me on, or remind me that my old-fashioned ways needed modernizing.

I sip my coffee, resigned to the fact that there will be no pleasant walks through the park today.

The first time I saw Maggie, she was sitting at a table in the university quad writing in a journal. Her hair—a brilliant, fiery-red—drifted loosely around her shoulders in the spring breeze. Her hand worked furiously, pen applied to page in such a dedicated manner that I was forced to stop and observe her. When she paused from her writing for a moment, I hoped that she would look at me, perhaps give me the chance to introduce myself. Instead, she looked past me, a dreamy quality to her gaze. Her eyes focused on something in the distance. She bit her lip and returned to her work in the journal without acknowledging that I was there.

I took to eating my sack lunch at a nearby table each day, always happy for the opportunity to catch another glimpse of her. I was a sophomore in college studying architecture. My mother still sent me off to school each day with a sandwich, a piece of fruit, and a thermos of watered-down coffee to get me through my afternoon classes.

I'd been sitting close to Maggie the day she spilled the contents of her bag. I rushed to her rescue, so breathless after collecting as many of her belongings as possible that I could barely respond to her cautious word of thanks. By some miracle, her student ID was one of the items that ended up in my hand. I stole a glance before handing it back to her and flushed with happiness, my heart thumping loudly in my chest at the way her name sounded when I spoke it long after she'd left me standing in the quad, alone. Her name was Margaret Adams.

Three weeks into our one-sided love affair, I knew that her friends called her Maggie, she was a graduate student, and she always ate three-fourths of her egg salad sandwich—bought from the vending machine in the union—before she picked the crust from what remained and balled the rest up in the cellophane wrapper. She preferred green apples over red, refused to eat a banana once the skin had begun to show spots of brown, and her beverage of choice was orange soda.

Maggie often wrote in her journal on her lunch break. When she wasn't writing, she was just as deeply involved in other books. She was an avid reader; the covers of her selections as varied as the brightly colored blouses she wore.

Years later, I would note the way her journal keeping progressed. The frequent, yet haphazard entries grew more habitual and regular. By 1987, she was journaling daily, often spending an hour or more before bed recording the details of the day. As years passed, her entries grew more specific in detail about people, places, and seemingly innocuous bits of information. We celebrated our seventh wedding anniversary that year, and our daughter, Lily, turned three.

"The girl was having seizures. Was it epilepsy?" Maggie is still reading her old journal at the kitchen table.

"Yes. Something like that. She outgrew it, though. They were less severe as she got older. By her teen years, she didn't have the seizures anymore."

Maggie lets out a rush of air, as if she's been holding her breath for too long.

"So she got better and I forgave you?" Her brow is furrowed in doubt.

"Yes. Our daughter grew up healthy and strong." I hope she doesn't ask the questions that always follow.

Where is she now? Can I see her? What does she do?

I change the subject.

"Are you hungry, Maggie? I'm going to fix myself a bowl of oatmeal for breakfast. Would you like one?"

I am pretty sure she'll refuse me. These days it is up to me to remember when Maggie is hungry. Her own mind doesn't pay attention to that little detail any longer. Left to her own devices, Maggie might never eat. She always claims she has just finished a meal, or she complains about being hungry and then forgets by the time a plate is put in front of her that she has asked for something.

She refuses my offer, and I fix her a bowl anyway. I sit it in front of her, place the spoon in her hand, and politely encourage her to eat.

"If I am your wife, perhaps I should be fixing breakfast for you."

This is the kind of statement that baffles me. The Maggie I love and married would never consider breakfast a wife's job. A nicety, perhaps, but never an obligation. She stands quickly and moves to the stove. As muddled as her mind has become, her body is still lithe and agile. She is both quicker than me and more sure on her feet.

Maggie fills a pan with water and sets it on the gas stove, turning the flame down a bit after the fire flares. For a moment, I can remember her competence. She moves to the pantry and pulls out the box of oats. Something catches her eye, however, and before long she is moving from cupboard to cupboard, searching. I listen to the click of cupboard doors and shuffle of dishes as she pulls items at random, looking beneath and behind for something she clearly cannot remember at this point. The water on the stove begins to boil. I turn the burner off. Maggie pulls a blue pitcher from the far cabinet in the corner and carries it to the table. She holds it up to the light, peering through it.

"I should make lemonade," she whispers.

This is the way it goes these days. I try to remember how long it has been since moments of true clarity were with us. It is such a gradual, wasting disease that it is hard to pinpoint a single moment of change. It makes me sad that I didn't recognize the last clear-headed day Maggie had, because I had no idea it would be the last. I feel my temper flare, helpless against the injustice of it all.

Maggie's mother likely also had early onset Alzheimer's disease, but she died in a car wreck shortly after Maggie and I met. The quirks of Maggie's mother's personality had not yet grown severe enough to be recognizable as anything inherently out of place.

Maggie wears a flustered look when I guide her back to the cooling bowl of oatmeal. Hands wringing in agitation, she finally focuses on me and grows fearful.

"Who are you?" she cries. "Where's nurse?"

For some reason, Maggie's mind is able to maintain the concept of nurse, a woman who comes daily to care for her. It doesn't seem to matter to Maggie that the actual person differs from day to day. They are sent by an agency. One comes from ten to noon, a second arrives around five to help Maggie settle in for the evening. I only requested once that one not come back. She was a heavy-set woman about our age. Her harsh scolding at Maggie's forgetfulness was unforgivable. She was rough while helping Maggie dress, and my wife had cried and whimpered at her touch. I am a paying customer with long-term prospects, so the agency works hard to keep me happy.

"Nurse will be here soon, Maggie. I'm here to care for you until she arrives. My name is George. Remember me? I'm your George."

This settles her for the moment. I watch her eat her bowl of oatmeal as my own grows cold in front of me. Today, it seems, we will not have the conversation about what happened to our daughter Lily when she outgrew those seizures. I will not have to relive the car wreck, so hauntingly near the very spot where Maggie's own mother lost her life. When this story is retold, it always seems to open a channel of memories. Her shock at hearing the gruesome end of her only daughter turns to grief as she recollects the details of her own mother's accident. These two incidents, years apart, are deeply tangled in Maggie's mind.

The facts of Maggie's condition were well documented by the time our daughter died, of course, and she had already stopped writing by then... at least, writing as the best-selling novelist, Margaret Adams Milhan. Maggie continued, on most days, to write feverishly in her journals. She always carried them with her and stopped multiple times per hour to capture what was happening in her life on paper. Our daughter, Lily, was so good with her mother. She was quick to recognize when Maggie was disoriented and was a natural at comforting Maggie in her worst moments.

The worst days now are the ones when Maggie searches the house for Lily. For a while, I felt compelled to be truthful with Maggie. I explained to her, time and again, that our daughter was dead. Last week when Lily was in Maggie's mind, I simply offered benign excuses. Our girl was at the library studying with friends. She had taken her brother to a movie. I even went so far as to fake a conversation with our daughter on the telephone, assuring her mother that she was safe on an overnight at a friend's house.

"Who are you?" Maggie asks as she scrapes the bottom of her bowl with her spoon.

"I'm George, Maggie. I'm your George."

I get up and clear the table, scraping my own untouched oatmeal into the trash. The vibration of the thudding bass of rock music travels through the floor. Maggie sits up straight in her chair and looks about as if expecting to see something slither across the floor.

"It's okay Mags. It's Jared. Our son. He's up now."

She looks at me blankly.

Jared begins singing, and I close my eyes for a moment, imagining us a normal family. I picture Maggie already hard at work in her office, steadily pounding the keyboard as she churns out her next bestseller. She completed six books before things got bad. We hired an assistant for the last two, though initially I had not understood that the help was medically necessary.

It was Maggie's agent who first encouraged me to take her to a doctor. She called me one morning at my office. Maggie was struggling with the outline of novel number five. It seemed to me an inordinately prolonged process, something that seemed to grow more difficult for Maggie with each passing book.

"Mr. Milhan, I'm worried about Maggie." The agent was blunt. "She sent me this outline for the next novel."

"Yes, she's been working pretty hard at this one."

"It's a repeat. This is novel number two all over again. Even some of the names are the same."

I tried to remember what Maggie's second novel had been about. I read them all so many times, so many drafts and versions in and out of order, that it was hard for me to keep up with what she had published and what was still in the works.

"Nah, same theme maybe. But Maggie wouldn't send you the same story."

"I'm telling you, this is novel number two. This isn't even close to what Maggie and I talked about. And when we spoke on the phone last week? She was incoherent. Mr. Milhan, is Maggie taking something?"

"Taking?"

"She's under a lot of stress. Her first book hit high and she's been a top-seller ever since."

"Are you accusing… That's crazy. You know Maggie is as clean as a whistle. She won't even have more than half a glass of red wine with her dinner."

"I'm just saying that something isn't right. You need to talk to her. Maybe you need to have her see someone. A specialist. Have her checked out."

I hung up the phone with that sinking feeling in the pit of my stomach. Maggie's agent had simply pointed out the obvious. Maggie wasn't herself. This was more than stress. This was more than fret over my leaving the firm to start my own business. It was more than being worried about our beautiful daughter, who was thankfully outgrowing her seizures by that time.

When I arrived home that day, I went straight to Maggie's office and looked around. Her desk was in shambles. There was a stack of papers, nearly a ream thick, beside the printer. I picked it up and looked at the first page.

> *My name is Maggie May Adams. I am Margaret Adams Milhan. My husband is George. My daughter is Lily. I am 35 years old. My name is Maggie.*

The second page was similar.

> *I am Maggie Milhan. I am married to George. I have a daughter, Lily. My mother died in a car wreck when I was 24. My mother was forgetful. She once set the curtains in the kitchen on fire while trying to cook eggs. She cried for hours. She cried because the curtains were ruined. She cried because she couldn't remember how to cook eggs. She cried because she couldn't remember my name. I think she forgot I was her daughter. My daughter's name is Lily.*

Page after page the notes went on, never more than a few sentences or, at most, a long paragraph. My blood ran cold. I couldn't begin to fathom what was happening. My lovely, bright, artistic Maggie who could pour words onto a page that flowed like a river was printing page after page of mindless dribble. *I am Maggie. I am Margaret Adams Milhan. George Milhan is my husband. I am married to George.*

The previous night, as was her habit, she'd been journaling in bed.

"George? What did we have for breakfast this morning? What was that you said about Lily? You said something funny. I wanted to remember it. What did you say George?"

I had been impatient with her. My habit was to catch up on the news before bed. Her constant interruptions kept me from a news article.

"Was it this afternoon that we took Lily to the fair?"

I tossed my magazine onto the floor in frustration.

"The fair? The fair was two weeks ago, Maggie. What are you talking about?"

"Two weeks?" She flipped back through the pages of her journal, lines of anxiety creasing her beautiful face. "Ah yes. Here it is. We took Lily to the fair."

It was at that moment I noticed the first streaks of silver hair at her temple.

"You're growing gray, Maggie."

She pulled her long auburn hair forward and examined the streaks. "Hmm," she sighed. "Must be getting old."

Maggie returned to writing in her journal. I rolled over and closed my eyes.

"And forgetful," I heard her murmur as I drifted off to sleep.

That day in Maggie's office, I felt my own hair growing gray. The words of her agent echoed in my mind as I sorted through the stack of papers, searching for something that would help it all make sense. I opened the top drawer of her desk. There was her typical stash of little round sour candies. She had always scolded herself for eating junk food while she wrote. There were four small packages in the drawer. I started to slide the drawer shut, then realized that each package was open. I dumped the contents of one on her desk. Only red candies remained. I dumped a second. Red again. I peeked inside the other two packages. Each contained only a handful of red candies apiece.

The trash bin beneath her desk was overflowing. There was a post-it note stuck to the bottom of her computer screen with instructions for shutting down the computer. Maggie had been using computers longer than anyone I knew. Perhaps, I reasoned, the instructions were for Lily. I knew Maggie sometimes let our daughter play games on her computer.

The room was messy. It was out of character for Maggie. Though I wouldn't typically have classified her as a particularly neat, orderly and generally tidy most definitely applied. Something about the smell of the room wasn't quite right. I sniffed until my nose led me to a bottom drawer where I found a slightly more than half-eaten sandwich type thing that I would have guessed was egg salad before it began sprouting various decorative fungi. I grabbed the trash basket and stuffed the overflowing papers in deep. As much as I didn't want to, I noted that many of them resembled the stack of papers by the printer. *I am Maggie. I am Margaret. My mother had trouble remembering.*

I dropped the moldy sandwich into the can. I went to the closet in search of a liner. Though I knew Maggie stored her journals there, I was a bit taken aback to see them lined up neatly on the shelves, years clearly marked on the spines. Some of the more recent years had multiple volumes. The current year, 1989, already had three.

I picked up a volume marked 1975-77. Maggie and I were dating then. There were lots of doodles and little quips about things people said or passages she recorded from books. There was a lengthy, heartfelt entry on the date of her mother's death. I was mentioned frequently. Her rock. The person who had kept her standing. I scanned the entries quickly, feeling an emotion well within me that I couldn't quite define.

I replaced the journal and pulled 1980, the year we got married. The entries were regular. Weekly, at least, with more mundane details of everyday life, but mostly just reports on significant events. There were practice runs at her side of the vows which we wrote ourselves and, on the day of our wedding, there was an extended entry about missing her mother. There were lots of thoughts about her writing career. Her second book was published that year and she signed the contract for three more the week before our wedding.

I ran my hand across the spines of 1982,1983, and 1984. I picked up 1985, somehow sensing that it felt heavier than the others. Not in sheer number of pages so much as in content. Sure enough, this journal began with a long and lengthy ramble about Maggie's state of mind. I read the opening lines a dozen times, committing them to memory.

> *On occasion, I find myself full-stride in the middle of my day when I suddenly have the sensation of waking for the very first time. I might become surprised by my surroundings, or by the fact that I have spaghetti cooking in a pot on the stove, or that this baby in my arms is of my own flesh and blood. It's as if a stranger has stepped in for a moment and taken over my body. And then, just as suddenly, that stranger steps away again and leaves me standing in a place that is*

not familiar. The act of waking is often joyful, but sometimes the act of waking fills me with great fear.

I flipped quickly through the pages. Entries were frequent, often daily. I tucked the journal into my jacket pocket, found the trash bag I'd originally gone searching for, and returned to Maggie's desk. I collected the sheets of paper, dropped to my knees to pick every last piece from the floor and added the stack from beside the printer. I stopped to take a breath, then selected a few sheets from the bag. I folded these and tucked them between the pages of the journal in my pocket. I dumped all the candies into the trash and stacked the remaining papers, the ones that looked somewhat novelish in value, in the center of the desk. I swept away the paper dust and staple remnants haphazardly with my forearm. I cleared the empty orange soda cans from the counter. I made a stack of dirty saucers, plates, silverware and mugs to be carried into the kitchen. Then I pulled out the phone directory and flipped it open to scan the list of physicians. I had no idea where to begin.

Maggie's shadow suddenly leapt across the desk at me. "There you are," she said from the doorway. "I have a surprise for you."

At that moment, she was so entirely and truly Maggie that I found it easy to shove aside my anxiety. She handed me a small, elongated box tied shut with a red ribbon. We hadn't exactly talked about having a second child, but the idea of one had been mutual, perhaps only put off in consideration of the seizures Lily suffered through toddlerhood, and the unspoken fear that something about our combination—Maggie and I—was broken, rendering us incapable of producing a healthy child.

Maggie was nearly three months along with our second child before my anxiety about her mental health returned. I came home from the office early one day to find smoke billowing from the microwave oven, the fire alarm sounding, unheeded, and Maggie placidly bleaching the sink without the protection of gloves. Lily, nearly six years old by then, cowered in a corner sobbing and sucking her fingers, obviously spent from what must have been heart-rendering cries at the start. I unplugged the microwave, which still showed twenty-four minutes of cooking time left, and carried the entire smoking heap into the yard.

I opened windows and turned on fans, pausing only long enough to scoop my daughter into my arms, shushing her and stroking her hair as I fought my desire to scream at my wife and shake her back to her senses. As the smoke began to clear, Maggie turned. A broad smile lit her face when she saw me. In a flicker, her expression turned to one of puzzlement, then worry as she seemed suddenly aware of the acrid smell that filled the house and our child's small body clinging to mine. Lily refused Maggie's comfort and simply turned her head away, hiccuping soft sobs against my neck.

As the doctor questioned me in a private meeting after his first thorough examination of Maggie, I became aware of just how long I'd been making excuses for her slips of mind, her occasional bouts of bad humor, her puzzled pauses and escapes into incoherent rambles. Maggie's recently hired writing assistant became more to us than any of us expected. I drew her into our circle of confidence in spite of Maggie's protests. Tabby was our first nurse maid, and thankfully skilled enough in organizing the written word that between them, two more books were to hit the best-seller list. Eventually, Maggie grew so sidetracked that she forgot, most days, that she was a novelist.

Jared, our son, finally bounds up the stairs, and I witness him stop in the doorway, taking a moment to assess his mother's condition before choosing his course. At seventeen, Jared has never really known his mother. He is a confident and well-adjusted boy in spite of the difficulties. He had his sister, Lily, for the first ten years and Maggie's assistant, Tabby, all along. I like to believe that I at least somewhat made up for his mother's sporadic attempts at bonding. Though Tabby officially left as our employee when Jared was about twelve, she is a continued influence in our lives. She stops to visit frequently with Maggie and even acts as her assistant on rare days when Maggie wakes to remember a looming deadline.

Tabby, now a published author in her own right, treats Jared as she would her own, much more a mother to him than Maggie was ever capable.

"Good morning, Momma," he swoops across the room and playfully pecks Maggie on the check. This brings a quick smile to her face, followed by a frown of puzzlement.

"Are you George?" she asks him.

"George is the old guy standing by the sink," he grins at me as he speaks. "I'm Jared."

"Are you Lily's boyfriend?" she asks.

Jared kneels beside his mother's chair and gently puts his arms around her.

"Lily and I," he says, pressing his forehead to hers. "Lily and I are, indeed, very good friends."

Maggie smiles at this and pats him awkwardly on the shoulder. From an early age, Jared has seemed to understand just what to say to make his mother happy. He endures her occasional tirades, which Tabby and I always struggled to protect him from, with solemn understanding.

"Would you like some lemonade?" she asks, springing from her chair with purpose in her step. She picks up the blue pitcher from the center of the table and fills it part way with water. She steps to the fridge and begins rummaging in the bottom drawer. I find myself wishing I had picked up lemons on the last trip to the store, though there was no way to predict when fresh-squeezed lemonade would be on the agenda.

I go to the cupboard and find some instant lemonade mix. She backs away with that puzzled, blank look on her face.

"Here's the lemonade, Maggie," I say. I fill the pitcher the rest of the way up and measure the right amount of powder. She takes the measuring cup from my hand and dumps the powder into the pitcher. I hand her a wooden spoon that she holds awkwardly. When she begins to stir, we watch the water swirl into a vortex, emptiness filling the space where sweet lemonade should have been. She stops, pours the drink into the three cups that I have put out on the counter, and picks up two. She turns around slowly, searching for her cue for what to do next. She spies Jared sitting at the table, downing an enormous bowl of cereal in the way that only a teenaged boy can. She carries the glasses to the table and sits one down in front of him. He thanks her and takes a polite swig.

She watches him eat. Her mouth twitches nervously. Her eyes dart from Jared to various points around the room. I can see her searching, yearning for a place to anchor her wandering mind.

"Are you the nurse?" she finally asks.

I chuckle. The one and only experience we had with a male nurse ended disastrously. Maggie beat him repeatedly with a fly swatter, swearing and cursing up a storm as she backed the poor, cowering kid—fresh out of school—into the corner of our walk-in closet. Tabby had arrived just in time to rescue him.

Jared smiles warmly at his mother. "I'm just Jared," he says with a shrug. "I'm Jared, and that's George. Two guys who love and care about you, Mom."

She spills her lemonade and begins to weep as I hurry to clean it up.

"I want nurse," she cries. "Where is nurse?"

"It's okay, Maggie." I try to assure her. "Nurse will be here soon." I glance at my watch and point to the minute hand. "Thirty minutes. Very soon. Nurse will be here for you soon."

Last year, Jared had his DNA tested to find out if he was likely to be afflicted with his mother's disease. I resisted, at first. In my mind, I could only imagine being handed a sentence, at the age of sixteen, for a mind that was bound to fail sooner than seemed fair. I couldn't imagine taking away my son's hope. I couldn't imagine robbing him of the endless possibilities I saw for his future. It was Tabby who talked sense into me.

"The sentence is already there," she told me. "Your boy has been reading about early-onset Alzheimer's disease since he's been able to read. He understands how great his risk is. He knows that this is likely carried in the genes and that he has a 50/50 chance of carrying that same gene his mother has."

"It's not that simple," I argued. "The doctors will tell you, it is not that easy and predictable."

"Imagine being a kid and knowing that your path would carry you one of two ways. If you knew for a fact that your mind was going to betray you by the age of 30, wouldn't that affect the choices you were going to make?"

"But there is no way to know. He could have a bad gene and be fine anyway."

"This is important to Jared. You have to let him take the test. He's been following the development of this technology since he was just a kid and he wants to know. Don't you think Maggie would have wanted to know?"

And this was the part that stumped me. Would Maggie have wanted to know? What would she have done differently? Would she have married me? Would she have given birth to our lovely Lily who only shared our world for sixteen years? Would Jared have even been a flicker in our hearts if Maggie had really understood what was happening to her?

In the end, I relented, and Jared discovered that he does not carry the gene, or any of the suspected genes, thought to be linked to his mother's dementia. In one year I've witnessed his confidence and spirits soar, though he was always a positive and friendly boy. He set his heart and mind on medical school. He started devouring college textbooks and following medical journals online the way I used to follow hip new techniques in building design and news on environmentally friendly construction materials.

He would have taken the test on his own eventually, but I thank Tabby in my heart every day for making me see reason.

A few weeks after Jared received his test results, we were watching a baseball game on television. He muted the sound and looked at me.

"Do you think that maybe Lily dying in that car wreck was a good thing Dad?"

A lump of anger and grief rose high in my throat.

"I can't imagine why you would say such a thing." My voice came out husky, shattered.

"I was just thinking about Mom and the way she is now, and I imagine Lily was just as scared of turning out like that as I was."

I thought of the diary tucked beneath my daughter's mattress. The pink and purple swirls on the cover. She wore the tiny gold key on a chain around her neck. It was not returned to us with the rest of her belongings. I still picture it stuck in a crevice of the wreckage of that car or perhaps rusting in the ditch where her life ended. I once walked the area on a cool spring morning, thinking that if I found the key, I could open the diary and take a peek at my lost daughter's thoughts. Though the flimsy latch would be easy to pick or break, I can't bring myself to deface the treasured book in such a manner. To this day, I admit to waking in the mornings and pondering the site of that accident. Had the choice of that particular curve been intentional? Had my daughter ended her own life after enduring a particularly painful week of watching her mother's mind fade? Did she choose that curve, the place where she knew her grandmother had died, intentionally? Could both cases have been written up as accidents by kind people who knew better than to damn souls to hell by making public what was easier swallowed as mere coincidence of timing and misfortune?

"No," I whispered. Maggie still danced before my eyes, waltzing with Lily across the kitchen with our beautiful daughter in her arms.

My son's hand grips my shoulder, and for a moment I think my very core will unravel.

"We have to do this, Dad. You know we have to," he says softly.

I force myself to suck in air. I will myself to expel it again.

"There's a blue trunk in the closet," I say. "I think her journals will fit, and it will be a good place to store them at the nursing home."

I lose myself in my own thoughts until I hear a heavy thud on the table. I open my eyes to watch my son as he methodically arranges the pages of his mother's mind in the simple wooden box.

When he is satisfied, he shuts the lid. It feels final. The closing of a life's story. The end of possibilities. There will be no new memories recorded from here on out.

I follow Jared into Maggie's bedroom. Once upon a time it had been our den, but we fixed it up special for Maggie a few years back. Her bed was partitioned in the back, a sitting room where the night attendant slept and kept watch was arranged for comfort and visitors. It has been a suitable facility for Maggie's care.

I pull the large, flat suitcase from beneath her bed. Ashley has labeled Maggie's undergarments and clothing exactly as the nursing home requested. I open the flap and study the girl's tidy handiwork. The list from the admissions packet lay on top of the neatly folded clothes, the suggested numbers of each type of clothing ticked off in purple ink.

I close the suitcase and carry it to the center of the room. Jared pulls the quilt off the bed, an old one Maggie's mother made when Maggie was just a girl. I pick up a box and begin to fill it with the framed family photographs that decorate her room. Jared pulls the canvas that his sister painted in high school from the wall. It was a more glorious version of a tree that once grew in our back yard, the one where I hung the tire swing so many years ago. Both Lily and Maggie spent hours swinging there.

We work in silence, in complete agreement about which knick-knacks, stuffed animals, and other personal items will go and which will stay. The nurse will remain at home with Maggie while Jared and I go to the nursing home and decorate her new room. We think it will be easier on her if familiar things already fill the place when she arrives.

Maggie is holding her nurse's hand and giggling when we let them know we are stepping out. Nurse nods. Maggie doesn't seem to notice. It is best that way, I think. I don't want her to remember this as the day I abandoned her, just in case her mind decides to maintain this memory. I don't want her to think I no longer love her.

Jared drives. We unload Maggie's things.

"Mom's going to be fine here," he says. My son stands in the center of the tiny room, surveying his arrangement of photos. "This is the right thing to do, Dad. I know that Mom would tell you, if she could, that this is the right thing to do."

I nod, giving myself no other option than to believe him. Maggie will be well-cared for here. They have a lovely garden we can walk in on the good days. Her doctors, my son, Tabby, the various nurses who have become like members of the family; they all agree that Maggie's mind has deteriorated to the point that the nursing home environment will be better for her.

Maggie will be fine.

The question is, will I?

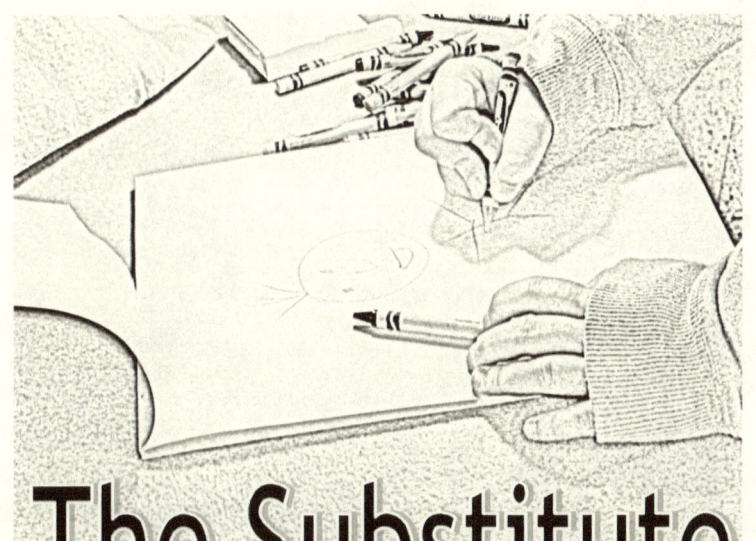

The Substitute

There was a substitute teacher my first day of school. I didn't know she was a substitute. She was Teacher as far as I was concerned. She was the most beautiful woman I had ever seen, and after only a day in her classroom, I believed she was the smartest woman, as well.

"Call me Mrs. Primrose," she said when she took my hand and led me into my first classroom.

Two days later, I was heartbroken to discover a stern old woman at the front of the classroom.

"Where's our teacher, Mrs. Primrose?" I asked the boy who sat across from me. I had not yet learned his name.

"This *is* the teacher," the boy said. "That other lady? She was just a substitute."

"What's a substitute?" I asked.

"Not a teacher," the boy said. "A substitute is someone they hire to watch the class when the teacher can't be there. A substitute can be just anyone."

That was when I learned that people weren't always what you assumed them to be, and that just anyone could be beautiful, kind, or brilliant, yet not get any recognition or credit for possessing those qualities.

Sometime later, Daddy and I saw Mrs. Primrose at the grocery store.

"It's my teacher!" I shouted. I ran to Mrs. Primrose and threw my arms around her legs.

"Well look who it is," Mrs. Primrose said. She gently patted my hair. She dropped to one knee in front of me and put a gentle hand on each arm.

"It's Katie Butterfield! I think you've gotten taller. How are you? How is school?"

She looked worried when I burst into tears. It worried me, too. I didn't understand why I was crying because I was so, so happy to see her again.

Daddy came up behind me and put his hand on my shoulder. He said hello to Mrs. Primrose. Then he apologized for my behavior, telling her that Momma was in the hospital and that it had been a difficult time for the whole family.

Mrs. Primrose invited us to the section of the grocery store where they sold sandwiches and sodas. She bought me a 7-Up with cherry syrup and an actual candied cherry in it. It was the most delicious drink I had ever tasted. Momma never let us drink soda.

We sat in tall chairs at an even taller table. My legs dangled, as there was nothing I could rest them on. I finally settled on sitting cross-legged in the chair, holding my pink 7-Up on my lap and drinking it slowly, relishing every bubbly sip.

Mrs. Primrose asked about my mother.

My father confessed things I had never heard before.

The cancer, he said, was why they sent Katie (that was me) to school early. My birthday was early September, but Momma hadn't thought I was ready to go. She had planned to keep me home for another year, but then the cancer came.

"I thought you were a local family," Mrs. Primrose said. "I wondered why she was starting school late in the year. How do you like kindergarten, Katie?"

I kind of wished she hadn't asked. Daddy got a funny look on his face when she said this. He looked like he was seeing me for the first time, like he'd almost forgotten I was sitting there.

"It's fine, Mrs. Primrose," I said. "But I don't like it near as much as I did when you were my teacher."

Mrs. Primrose smiled, and she and Daddy went back to talking like I wasn't there, so I studied the bubbles in my pink 7-Up very hard and pretended I wasn't paying attention to a word that they were saying.

On the inside, I promised myself that I would remember every detail.

Daddy talked quieter now, and I felt his eyes on me each time he looked in my direction. I ignored him as best I could. I pretended real hard to be fascinated by the bubbles in my drink. He told Mrs. Primrose that my momma's cancer was stage three.

Mrs. Primrose said a three was terrible, but beatable.

Daddy said that Grandma, my momma's momma, had the cancer, too. The cancer was what killed her.

When he said this, I forgot that I was studying the bubbles and not listening. "Is Momma going to die?" I asked, the tears I had just managed to get myself over were threatening to return.

Mrs. Primrose put her hand on my shoulder. She squeezed, and I put my drink on the table. I held my breath and leaned over until my head was resting on her lap.

"Your Momma is getting the best treatment there is," she said, her voice soft and whispery. "Her doctors are taking mighty fine care of her, and I bet seeing you every day does her a world of good, as well."

I didn't want to let myself breathe again. I was afraid that if I did, everything that was keeping me there in my body was going to spill out with my air and I would leak into pieces all over the grocery store floor. I squeezed my eyes shut tight and let the air go in tiny bits, in and out my nostrils.

Mrs. Primrose started talking about nice things, like the tulips she had planted in her yard and her yellow kitten whose name was Duckie.

"Would you like to come visit me sometime, Katie?" she asked. "We could make cookies that you could take home to your mom. We could paint with watercolors. You could help me pick the vegetables in my garden."

It sounded wonderful, so I nodded my head as hard as I could without lifting it, and still without opening my eyes. Daddy finally picked me up and carried me out of the store. I must have fallen asleep. I don't remember the car ride home. I don't remember him carrying me into the house and tucking me in bed.

My big brother, Ben, played football on the middle school team. He was a good athlete and also really smart in his schoolwork.

Grownups always told me how lucky I was to have a big brother like Ben.

When he came home from football practice, his clothes would be all damp with sweat. He'd put his helmet on my head, and I would laugh, even though it was kind of hot and damp and smelly in there. The day after Daddy and I saw Mrs. Primrose at the grocery store, I followed Ben into his room after he got home from football practice.

"Did you know Momma has cancer?" I asked.

Ben looked at me, and his face was very sad. I thought maybe he even looked scared, which didn't seem possible, and it made me even more scared than I was before.

"It's okay, Katie," he said. "Lots of people get cancer, and the doctors know how to fix it. Mom is sick, but she's going to get better."

Then Ben turned away from me, and I thought he might be crying. When I asked him if he was, he yelled at me. He told me to go away. To leave him alone.

I went to the kitchen and poured myself a glass of milk. I got a straw from the drawer and sat at the table, blowing bubbles into the white liquid. I studied those bubbles with every ounce of concentration I could muster. I blinked them away when they threatened to jump onto my eyelids.

Later that night, Ben came out and sat on the couch with me. He never said he was sorry for yelling, but he put his arm around me and we watched television. I stared at the screen as hard as I could, but when I glanced at my brother, I thought that he was probably staring at it even harder.

That's when I learned that people don't have to talk to make each other feel better.

I visited Mrs. Primrose on Momma's chemotherapy days after school. One weekend I stayed overnight with her and the yellow kitten. He had a very loud purr, and I liked lying on the floor at her house, letting him sit on my chest and vibrate my bones with his content.

One day at school, I got so mad about the boring story our teacher Ms. Pitts was reading to us, I told her that I hated her, and

I wasn't going to come to her class anymore. It was a bold and daring thing to say. I'm not sure I'd ever directly spoken to Ms. Pitts before that moment. I marched out of the classroom, determined to make good on my promise, and I listened to the class titter and exclaim their awe at what I had said.

The principal met me as I was on my way out the door to the school. He put a hand on my shoulder. He invited me into his office and he let me do numbers on his calculator machine. Daddy came and picked me up early. The next day he made me return. I pretended nothing happened, and much to my relief, Ms. Pitts seemed content to do the same.

School was over in May, and Ben and I spent a lot of time together that summer. He took me roller skating at the park. He taught me how to ride a bike. We both went to Mrs. Primrose's house where we picked vegetables that she sent home with us to eat.

In the fall, Ben went to high school and I started the first grade. I saw Ms. Pitts on the first day of school in the hallway, and she smiled at me and asked, "How was your summer, Katie?" I wanted to stick my tongue out at her, but I only shrugged and said, "Fine."

Momma was getting better, and the better she got, the less I saw of Mrs. Primrose.

Years later, Momma asked me what I remembered about the time when she was sick with cancer. She said I told her daily stories, of a woman named Primrose, and that my stories were so fanciful and lovely she always expected I was making them up.

I told Momma that I fancied up the stories because I thought they would make her feel better. The funny thing is, I have no memories of telling stories to Momma at all during that time. When I think of my mother during the cancer, I can only see the face of the substitute, Mrs. Primrose. I have memories of Daddy and Ben and Ms. Pitts … and my wide-eyed view of the classroom at school. I remember Duckie, the yellow kitten, and I remember bubbles in pink soda and white milk.

Of my mother, I have no recollection at all.

In America

"Mr. Sam! Mr. Sam!" Jorge calls out cheerfully as he bolts across my garden, skipping over the rows of carrots and radishes and pausing briefly to examine some beets.

"Morning, Jorge." I shake the dirt off a glove and wave to the boy as he slides a red backpack from his shoulders and sits it carefully between the rows of green and yellow pepper plants. Unzipping the pack, he nearly folds himself in, head first, searching for something. Out comes the yellow, tattered copy of *Curious George*.

I take the book. "You read it?"

"Every word." Jorge speaks in careful English and nods his head. "I read it to my mother, and she read it to me."

"She read it?"

"Yes, Mr. Sam. She is learning well. I am teaching her."

"I bet you are. Good for you, Jorge. Teach her well."

Jorge holds the book out to me.

"Another? Do you have another book I could read?"

I take the book from the child's brown hands. Dee read this one to our sons hundreds of times. I rub the cover with my fingers, feeling her there, worn spots made by her hands.

Dee is gone.

The boys have moved away.

The grandkids were never really interested in books anyway. The age for *Curious George* passed quickly. The last time my grandson visited, he spent his time text messaging, whatever the hell that is, a girl he loves in California. Two days with his grandfather in the summertime and all the boy could do was stare into some electronic gadget and bemoan the fact that he wasn't with his friends on the beach.

"You keep the book." I pass it back to Jorge. "Come by after school. I've got some more you can have."

The yellow school bus rolls slowly up the road.

"Better scat."

Jorge runs, leaps over my straight rows two by two.

"Thanks, Mr. Sam. I love the books. I will keep reading them."

The red backpack flops against the boy's brown arms. I chuckle.

"Quick, Jorge!"

His hand flies into the air, a casual wave in my direction as he stumbles into line. Eleven children gather at my corner, more than most of them brown-skinned and dark-headed like Jorge.

After forty-some years of the school bus stopping at my corner, I don't even try to plant grass there anymore. A few spindly weeds spring up in the summertime, but the rest of the year the ground is so trod by children's tennis shoes, scratching in the dirt like so many baby chicks, that it stands bare. Even the winter snows cannot hide the indentation made by the daily huddle of kids waiting for the school bus.

The old guys, with all their bellies aching and their knees going bad, have been urging me for years now to leave my place, move up north of town. For fifty years I've lived at the corner of 4th and Pine. It's true, things have changed. The old neighbors, the white ones, have mostly died or bought houses elsewhere. The new neighbors don't speak English, or, like Jorge, they speak with a musical lilt and new emphasis.

They've taken over the houses on Pine Street. Whole families of brothers, sisters, and cousins, maybe aunts and uncles, crowding into spaces once built for fewer people. The city is passing ordinances now. No more mobile homes parked in the back and side yards. No cars on blocks in front. No butchering of animals in the yards. There's talk of allowing English only to be spoken in the hallways of the school.

We'll fix it all with more rules.

But this is where they came first, Pine Street, once a nice, respectable neighborhood. Now I hear it called El Barrio, and the old guys tell me to get out while the getting is good.

Sure, they are different. Yet, they are very much the same. At least, it seems that way to me when I remember what we used to be… we "white-folk" with our "holier than thou" attitudes.

Beautiful children. The Mexicans love their kids. They throw elaborate parties. Colorful. Balloons and streamers. Cakes and sweets. Jorge's mother sent over em-pan-somethings on Jorge's eighth birthday. I had declined an invitation by Jorge's father, a gesturing wave from across the yard. I'd been watching too closely, relatives and friends, I assume, gathering in the driveway next door. I hadn't meant to look like I was spying. I don't believe in minding my neighbor's business. I'd just been mesmerized, for a moment, by the song of voices I could not understand, the array of bright color… the liveliness.

I retreated to my garden, finding numerous details that needed attending to, and then Jorge had appeared, smiling brown face of a boy with a plate of pastries. Good. Oddly sweet. Nothing like anything Dee ever made.

Me and the boy, Jorge, we are friends now.

This is not a fact I admit to the guys at the lodge where I still spend my Friday evenings reminiscing with the dwindling crowd. I listen to the young guys bitch and moan about the place being overrun by Mexicans. Not that many of the local sons are eager to work at the packing plants. The ones who do, most of them are in management positions. It's good money, I understand. Hard work, sure, but since when was that something to complain about.

A few of them have mingled enough to pick them up a pretty Latino girl. Yet, they criticize their sisters who've found boyfriends in the same families. Even more, the girls who have dared to have children – pretty little things who will grow up knowing both languages and maybe erase these lines we've drawn across this small Kansas town.

Double standards are the norm now. It's not okay. Yet, it's happening. Men my boys' ages, it seems hardest on them. But their sons and daughters are more accepting. No less racist, perhaps, but more open to the change and the growth it is bringing to our town.

Keith, one of the regulars at the lodge and an old neighbor, gave me a homemade sign on a stick. It read "No Venir Aqui."

"That's Spanish," Keith had explained, "Telling them Mexicans to stay out of your yard."

I accepted it graciously. I listened to the laughter, received their pats on the back. It's in the back of my garage, facing the wall behind some tools. I don't want Jorge to see it. I don't want to talk to him about the differences between my people and his people when we are getting on so well.

Jorge's mother has a name I can't seem to wrap my tongue around, no matter how hard I try. L-O-U-R-D-E-S. I made the boy write it down, exasperated as I listened to him repeat the name dozens of times, a delightful note dancing from his tongue. I keep the paper tucked in my wallet. I call her Mrs. Ramirez, though I'm pretty sure the boy gave me three or four names the first time he introduced her.

I am delighted by the beauty of Mrs. Ramirez in a way that deeply embarrasses me. She is a little on the short side, soft. She looks the way a woman should... none of this buns-of-steel, abs like six-packs that my daughters-in-law aspire to. Her long black hair falls neatly to her waist and her eyes are black and glitter like stones. She has a shy, easy smile. As far as I can tell, she speaks no English. She listens intently as I offer her tomatoes and peppers from my garden or as I trim the hedge that separates our yards, but always calls on the boy, Jorge, for interpreting.

"My mother says thank you very much for the tomatoes, Mr. Sam," Jorge will say. "My mother says she make you tamales for gift."

Jorge passes the dishes and buckets between our hands.

Alone in my kitchen, I eat her sweets and tamales made with so much corn meal. I sample flavors new to my tongue. I think of Dee and wonder how she would react, if she would caution me about accepting gifts of food or worry that the items might be undercooked or otherwise unfit for consumption.

I think that Mrs. Ramirez is a very skilled cook, likely with as much talent as my Dee had. It's not pot roast or that wonderful casserole made from green beans, but it is good food and my mouth waters for more.

Jorge's father, lucky for my unskilled tongue, is also named Jorge. Pronounced Hore-Hay. Easy enough.

Jorge Senior, as I think of him, is soft-spoken, but bold in his efforts to speak English, like his son. He often meets me at the end of the drive when we check our mailboxes. He works the late shift at the packing plant, hopes to move to days soon, and wants to work his way into a better-paying position now that he is legal and his family is here. He tells me of six years that he came across the border without permission, working migrant farm jobs and packing plants across Texas, Kansas, and Nebraska. All his money was sent home to support his family.

"It was easy then," he tells me. "No taxes. No utility bills. All cash. Lots of cash. Now my wife want new towels at the JC Penny store and my son want a computer with the Internet. We have car payment. House payment. Buy new furniture now, pay thirty days later. Is difficult. All the money goes to bills and cable and a big screen TV… and taxes."

We laugh. In taxes, we have common ground to grumble about.

When I trim the grass where our yards meet, Jorge Senior often comes out and trims his side at the same time. We work, side-by-side, not speaking. Often I feel him watching me for many minutes before he finally asks a question. I wonder if he is aware that I watch him, as well.

Sometimes it's the weather. Occasionally we discuss cars. Jorge Senior drives an old Ford truck, an early 90s model, but he'd really like a new one. Blue, he says.

Once he asked me about the church I attend. "You Catholic?" he asked.

"Lutheran," I answered.

"Brown church? Little? Down Chestnut Street?"

"Yeah, that's it."

"We're Catholic," he says. "All Mexicans. Catholic."

I laugh. "Yeah, we Lutherans were once Catholic, too. Some say we're not so different." Dee would've knocked me upside the head for making such a statement.

I detect skepticism in the look he gives me. He probably knows I have not left my home on a Sunday morning in all the time he has lived next door. His family, every Sunday, and Wednesday nights as well, they dress like they are going to some big shin-dig, a wedding. Jorge's little sisters are like princesses in tiny gowns of white and yellow.

Today, Jorge Senior sits on his front steps. His baby girl, Miranda, toddles out into the yard, swipes a dandelion, and returns to his knees. There is a pile there, yellow flowers on his legs and scattered on the ground beneath his boots. He waves at me and I wave back. I've tended the garden picture-book-perfect. There's not a grass to trim or a hedge to even in my yard. I slip my hands into my pockets and stroll his way. There is a folding chair tipped over in the grass. I pull it up alongside and sit. Miranda smiles for me and shyly offers her father's dandelion. I take it from her chubby brown hand.

"Buenos Dias. Nice day," Jorge Senior greets me.

I try to repeat his greeting, but it drops from my tongue and dribbles down my chin. I'm too old, or too dumb, to speak his language, so I sit, mute, feeling more awkward than I thought I might.

Jorge watches Miranda and twirls a dandelion stem between his fingers.

"Sam Mueller," he says my full name flatly.

There is a long stretch when the only sound is the murmur of the little girl. I don't know if she is just making noises, babbling, or speaking actual words in Spanish.

"Sam Mueller," Jorge Senior turns his eyes from his daughter to my face. "You Mexican? You have a Mexican abuela? Your wife? She was Mexican?"

"No!" I answer too quickly, too sharply. I sit forward in my chair and lean back again. "No," I say more quietly. "My people were mostly German, from Germany, a couple of generations back."

Jorge Senior's eyes glint dark and his brow furrows. He kicks his heel in the dirt, smashing small yellow flowers beneath his boot.

"Germany," he stretches the word with his teeth clinched. I think he is mimicking my pronunciation. He repeats the country of my people's origin, this time the music of his true voice ringing through. "You speak?"

"German? No." I shake my head.

"Your parents?"

I shake my head again, but then switch to a nod. "My father. He spoke German with his mother. She died when I was young. Five. I never heard him speak a word of German after that."

A shadow crosses Jorge's face. He looks to his daughter, Miranda.

"My children," he says softly. "My children speak Spanish very well."

I nod, not knowing what else to do.

"My grandchildren?" He shrugs.

Miranda dances a little circle and falls on her diaper padded bottom. She grins up at her father and he laughs.

"Sam," he states my name and waits for me to make eye contact. "Your father's mother. She proud her grandchildren speak English?"

"I suppose." I think of my grandmother. She was a hard woman, thick and unsmiling. She scolded if my siblings or I touched the cake batter pan, but would slip butterscotch candies to us from her apron pockets before sending us away with a thump on the head or a sharp tug to the ear.

"You think of your life if your grandparents had stayed in Germany?"

"No," I spoke with certainty. "Never do. Never consider it. It was different times, Jorge. Different times."

He watches me closely as I watch his daughter dance around his knees. When I find the nerve to meet his eye, he smiles.

"You're different, Mr. Sam Mueller. I thought maybe you had Mexican blood in you."

This time I feel flattered. I twirl a dandelion and get up, take a slow walk back to my own yard.

"You're a good neighbor, Sam Mueller," Jorge's voice carries across the yard.

Miranda waves a chubby hand in my direction. I wave back at the two of them. Lovely. Father and child. Sunny morning. Playing in the yard.

Occasionally, most often in the grocery store, I see Mrs. Ramirez in town. I always smile and tip my hat, and she rewards me with a smile in return. This morning she is standing near the counter at the convenience store. She and Maria, the girl who sells us old white guys strong coffee and cigarettes every weekday morning, are speaking rapidly in Spanish.

Ed, an enormous man in striped blue overalls, hoots and says, "What the hell they talking about? Don't they know this is America?"

"Hey! This is America!" Stanley yells, causing more than one of us to jump. "Don't you know that in America we speak English?" He's likely been adding some whiskey to his coffee, even though it's not yet nine in the morning.

My eyes fall to the table. I scrub at an invisible spot with my thumb, the words I should say sticking to the back of my throat. The lively chatter of Lourdes and her friend falls silent. I force myself to lift my eyes and look around. The men are laughing, already on to their jokes and musings, sure that one of them is the subject of the conversation between these two lovely ladies.

Keith starts with the lewd suggestions. He tells us a story of a hot Mexican momma and makes all kinds creative references to chi-chi's, cha-cha's, and hot tamales. My face burns. I clench my fist beneath the table.

"Enough." It's such a mumble that only the two men sitting closest to me are aware that I've said anything. Stanley looks at me curiously. I stand and say it forcefully, "Enough!"

Ed doesn't stop his story, but kind of sputters when he realizes I am not laughing.

Mrs. Ramirez keeps her eyes focused on the floor, but her friend, Maria, glares into the crowd of white old men with contempt. She keeps her head held high, her shoulders square.

I picture myself making a speech that shames them all. Calling to memory their mothers and grandmothers who brought them here, who made their lives in this country possible. It wasn't so long ago for most of us. I want to remind them of the tombstones in the Lutheran cemetery. How many inscriptions are not in English, but German?

Instead, I pick up my empty coffee cup. I toss it in the trash can as the bell on the convenience store door jingles, marking my exit for a now-silent crowd.

I don't realize she has left the store behind me until I've started my truck and shifted into reverse. She's standing there, her eyes the color of rich chocolate. Her fist is lifted, about to knock on my car window. I press the brake firmly and roll the window down without thinking.

I don't know what it is she wants to say, but after a moment of seeming to search for words, she says, "Good morning, Meester Sam Mueller." She speaks as if she is afraid of the words, of the way they might sound falling from her mouth.

"Good morning, Mrs. Ramirez. You can call me Sam."

"Good morning, Sam." This time her voice is stronger, the quiver from just moments before is gone. "You call me Lourdes."

It's that sound again, the one that makes my tongue curl round itself. I say it anyway, though it doesn't sound nearly so pretty in my old, white, American way of speaking.

She ducks her chin, shyness returns to both of us.

We are neighbors, she and I, in this country where I am old and she is new. I slip a butterscotch candy from my chest pocket, and pass it to her through the open window.

Jared Loves Allison

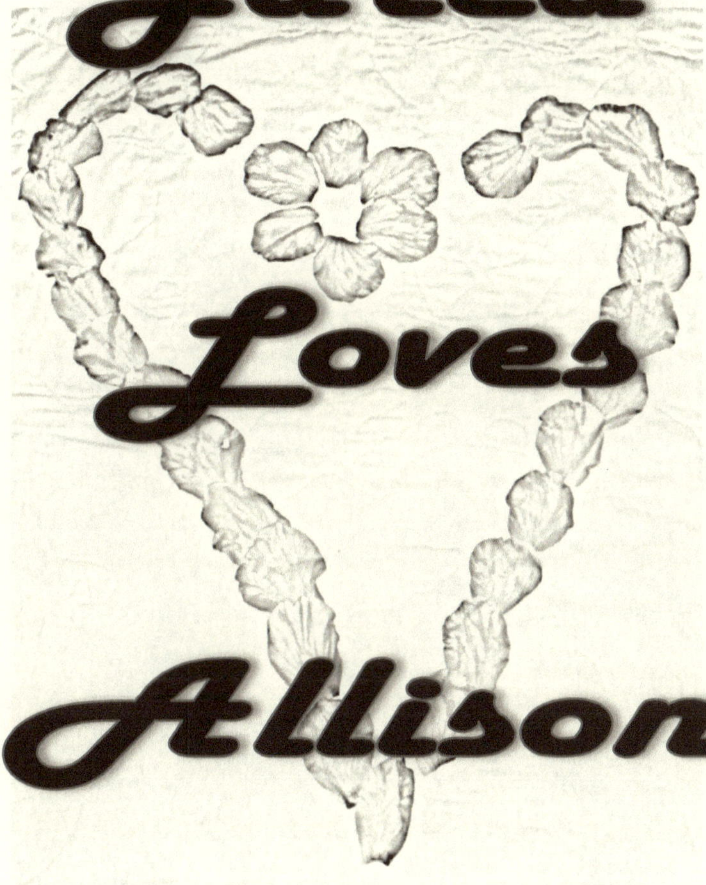

*J*ared turned the tiny box slowly, poking it with one slender finger. The box was gold with a pattern of linked hearts he could feel if he ran his finger slowly and gently over its surface. He pulled the ring from its slot and slipped it on his little finger. He knew the ring would fit Allison. The ring her parents gave her for Christmas fit his little finger in exactly the same way.

The diamond was large, though not as large as Jared had hoped for. The ring he had his eye on would have required another year, at least, of saving. His entire account was empty now, all of his money spent on this ring—everything he had earned in two and a half years at the Burger Barn, plus the five years' worth of birthday money from his grandparents.

A three-emerald cluster lay on each side of the diamond. It looked like a flower to Jared. The diamond was the bloom, and the emeralds were the petals. Emerald was Allison's birthstone—just barely. She was born on the last day of May.

Allison was a Gemini and Jared was a Cancer. They were not an ideal fit, according to astrological charts, but Jared didn't believe in that stuff anyway. He didn't see how birthdays could have anything to do with love and compatibility.

Jared closed his eyes and prayed—even though he'd grown up in a house that didn't teach him to pray, and he wasn't exactly sure that he was doing it correctly—that Allison would say yes.

He heard his father stirring in the bedroom downstairs. Jared pulled the ring off his finger and put it back into the box. He slipped the treasure into the front pocket of his backpack.

Jared got a bowl from the cabinet and a carton of eggs from the fridge. He began cracking eggs. His father would be upstairs soon and they would have breakfast together before leaving the house, his father for work, and Jared for school.

His dad tried to talk Jared into spending his money on a car this past summer, but Jared knew he was saving his money for Allison's ring, and his bike already got him everywhere he needed to go. When it didn't, a parent, Allison, or another friend could usually be found to give him a ride.

Jared was heating the skillet and beating the eggs when his father's footsteps hit the basement stairs.

"Good morning!" his father sang.

"Hey, Dad," Jared answered. He appreciated his father's melodious way of expressing himself, especially early in the morning, even though he was always slightly off tune.

His father pulled a loaf of bread from the cupboard and placed four slices in the toaster. With his father, Jared always ate wheat bread, the seventy-seven-cent generic brand loaf from the supermarket. Jared's mom was into more exotic stuff from the bakery with amazing smells and intriguing names like tomato-basil, pumpernickel rye, and wheatberry. Jared preferred his father's plain breads, but he ate his mother's fancy breads when she was the one fixing the meals.

Jared's father went to the fridge and pulled out a block of sharp cheddar. He stood beside Jared and grated cheese into the skillet as Jared pushed the eggs around with a spatula. Jared noted that their shoulders were touching. He breathed deeply and smiled, thinking of his last mark on the doorjamb. He was now a full inch taller than his father, a fact that still struck him as absurd and a bit amusing.

"So, have you given any more thought to my proposal?" his father asked.

"Yeah, I really don't think I want to go," Jared said, stirring the eggs with renewed focus.

"Forgive me, Jared, but is there something I am missing? How can you turn down a free trip to Europe?"

"I just don't think I want to go, Dad," Jared said.

"Is it Allison? She'll still be here when you get back, you know." His father was shaking his head.

Jared remained silent. Of all the talks he'd had with his father, this was the one he knew his father would never understand.

Jared's dad stuck the grater in the dishwasher and pulled two plates from the cabinet. He rummaged through the silverware drawer.

"It's your high school graduation, Jared. I just want to give you something special. You're a teenager. You should have a list a mile long of things you want to do and see.

"Yeah, and going to Europe isn't on that list," Jared replied, attempting to keep his voice even.

"Why not? It's an experience I would have killed for when I was your age."

"What can I say? I'm not you, okay?"

"Jared, look. I'm not trying to tell you what to do with your life. I just want to give you a nice graduation gift, okay?"

"Then get me a car," Jared said. "It's something I could really use, okay? A car."

His father sighed deeply and sat down at the table, sorting the silverware between Jared's place and his own. "Your mother is getting you a car," he said. "Don't tell her I told you."

Jared pulled the eggs from the fire and turned off the heat. He walked to the table and tipped the skillet, pushing scrambled eggs onto each plate.

"Just help Mom pick out the car, Dad. Help her pay for it. That will be enough."

"Jared, your mom has her own money. She doesn't need my help paying…"

"It's not about need, Dad," Jared said, his voice rising. "It's about the way things are supposed to be."

"Listen, we don't need to yell to talk about this," his father said.

"I'm not yelling!" Jared said, making a strong effort to bring his voice back to normal pitch. If there was anything his father hated, it was discussion carried on in less than civilized tones.

His father ate a bite of eggs in silence, and then said, "We forgot the toast and the coffee."

Jared got up and tossed the toast back to the table. He pulled coffee cups from the rack and poured two, leaving plenty of room for cream and sugar in his own. He favored his father on bread selection, but his mother on coffee. From her cabinet, he pulled a tall jar of powdered, flavored cream. He didn't care which flavor today, as long as it would cut down on the bitter taste of black coffee.

"So tell me," his father's voice was low and calm. "Just how are things supposed to be?"

Jared turned and looked at his father. Overhead, he heard the floor squeak. This meant his mother was beginning her morning ritual of yoga and meditation. She would be down in time to see him off before he headed to school.

"This," Jared said, gesturing to the ceiling and then to the basement stairs. "My father and mother should be sleeping in the same bed, not on two completely different floors of the house."

"Oh geezus," his father said. "Not this again."

"My parents should be buying me a graduation present *to-geth-er*," Jared said. "Together, Dad. One present from one set of parents. That's the way it's supposed to be."

"I thought you'd gotten over this years ago," his father said. "You should be happy that you have two parents who love you. You have more than most, Jared. You have friends at school who would give their right arms for a life like yours. Your mom and I? We've done well by you."

Jared knew he couldn't argue with that. His father was right. He thought of all his friends that lived in single parent homes. Some of them had little to no contact with a second parent. Hell, some had little to no contact with a first. Far too many had lives spent being buffers between two people who hated each other.

Jared knew he couldn't explain to his father why he sometimes envied those kids. Maybe their parents hadn't been reasonable, but at least they had been passionate. Where there was hate, there must have once been love.

"Your mother and I chose to be your parents," his father said, his expression soft as he gazed at his son. "We made the rational decision to be the best parents we could be for you. We didn't let anything stand in the way of that. Not even each other."

"Why not marriage?" Jared said, feeling defeated already.

"Marriage?" His father spoke carefully. "Do you really believe a little certificate bestowed upon a couple from the county courthouse is going to guarantee happily-ever-after? People don't stay married, Jared. A marriage certificate doesn't prove commitment."

"It's not just a certificate, Dad," Jared said. He felt himself getting emotional, not a route he wanted to take with his father.

"What difference would it have made to you if your mother and I were married?"

Jared looked at his father.

"We'd have both attended your little league games? Oh wait, we did that. We'd have both gone to school conferences? Oh wait, we did that, too. We'd have both tucked you in each night and chased the monsters from under your bed? Oh wait…"

"You did that. You did that. I know," said Jared.

Jared's mother appeared in the doorway. "What on earth is going on here?"

"Our son is trying to tell me why his life would have been better if you and I were married," his father said.

"No, it's not that," Jared said, flustered and angry.

"Oh Jared," his mother said. "We've been over this before. You know how hard your father and I have worked to do what's best for you."

Now that Jared's mother was here, he knew there'd be no controlling his emotions. "Second best, maybe," Jared said, standing as his face grew bright with anger. "Second best is maybe what you've given me. What Allison has. That's best!"

"And what's that? Constant entertainment from the ongoing bickering?" His father's voice dripped with sarcasm.

"Her parents love each other!" Jared said.

"Love? But you say they fight all the time," his father answered.

"They fight. And then they make up." Jared's face was growing hot, and he fought to get the words out. "They argue, and they kiss, and they make up. They hold hands. They hug each other. They laugh together."

"We laugh..." his mother looked as if she had been slapped.

"Not together!" Jared stepped back from the table and began to pace. "There's you and me, or me and Dad. There is no us! We have no family."

"Oh, come on, Jared. You're being unreasonable," his mother said.

"Would you really rather your parents be unfulfilled in a loveless marriage than..."

Jared cut his father off. "Why couldn't you just love each other? For my sake?"

"Your father and I care deeply about each other," his mother answered.

"But it's a calculated relationship," his father finished her sentence. "We chose to be your parents, first. We didn't want the complications of marriage to get in the way of that."

"Complications?" Jared wanted to choke the reason out of his father.

"Do you really think Allison's mother is happy?" his mother asked.

"What makes you think she isn't?" Jared turned on her.

"The woman works as a clerk in a discount store," his mother answered.

"Maybe there is more to her life than work," Jared returned.

"Jared, think about what you are saying," his father said.

"I am thinking. I think about it all the time."

"Then you know you are being silly about this. You're nearly eighteen. You're graduating from high school in a couple of weeks. We've given you a good life here, a good start," his mother said, her agitation with him clear in her speech.

"Look, I just wanted to get you a nice graduation gift," his father said.

"And that's fine," Jared said as he tried to calm his jagged breathing.

"Then what is this all about?" His mother came forward and touched his arm.

"Nothing. Everything is okay. I'm okay. And you guys are obviously great. I don't know what I was thinking, except that I don't want to go to Europe. Keep your tickets, Dad. Keep your gift."

"Nobody said that you had to go to Europe," his mother said, throwing a stern glance in his father's direction.

His father shrugged. "I never said he had to. I just thought he might want to. I wanted to get him a nice graduation gift. That was all. That's what started this whole thing."

Jared picked up his coffee cup and headed for the bathroom. He turned on the cold water and began rinsing his face. He was exhausted. He glanced at his watch. He had less than fifteen minutes before his dad would be leaving to drop him off for school.

He looked at himself in the mirror. He had his father's nose and his mother's blue eyes. They were right. They had always been there for him. They had given him more than most kids his age ever got, even those whose parents had been married for their whole lives. Maybe he was making too much of this. Maybe it had been a mistake to buy Allison that ring.

His heart seized with that thought. He couldn't imagine a day without Allison. He dreamed of living, not on separate floors of the same house with her as his parents did, but truly with her. He wanted to share everything about his life with Allison, his job, his bedroom, himself. Jared wanted to marry Allison more than anything else in the world. He wanted it more than college or even high school graduation. He certainly wanted it more than a passport to Europe. He just wanted to love her and have her promise that she'd love him—forever, till death did them part and all of the other stuff that came with that little certificate.

He thought back to his childhood. He remembered a time when he did not realize that what he had was unusual. He remembered the moment he understood that other kids' parents did not date other people, at least, not when they were married, and certainly not when they lived in the same house. He supposed that did make him special, but he only hated that it made him different. He hated the things the kids at school would say about his mom and his dad, things he knew their parents said about his family. He had parents that lived together, but behaved like people who lived apart. People didn't understand that. The older Jared got, the less he understood it.

What he wanted, more than anything, was two parents who loved each other. Not just two people who planned and coordinated well, and would more than likely move their separate ways once he was grown and out of the house. He wanted parents who were married, even if marriages could not be expected to last. And if he couldn't have that, he would at least give that to his own children.

Jared went back into the kitchen and picked up his backpack. His father was getting his jacket from the closet and his mother was spreading cream cheese on a whole wheat bagel. She placed the bagel on the counter and went to Jared. She wrapped her arms around him and squeezed hard. Jared rested his chin on top of his mother's head and hugged her back.

He pulled the backpack, slung from one shoulder, up under his arm and let his hand rest on the pocket where the little box was stored.

"Ready to go?" his father asked.

"Yeah, I just got to get something out of my room," Jared said.

He went to his room and unzipped the pocket of his backpack. He carefully placed the ring in his sock drawer where it would wait until the evening of graduation.

"I hope she says yes," he whispered.

Allison was laughing with her friends next to her locker. Jared caught her eye with a wave and she smiled. His heart quickened when she skipped away from her friends and toward him.

"Guess what?" she was practically squealing with delight.

"What?" Jared kissed her quickly since public displays of affection were against school rules.

"My parents gave me my graduation present early," Allison said with a giggle as she fished an envelope from her bag and presented it to Jared.

He carefully opened it and pulled out a plane ticket.

"I leave the day after graduation. There's a whole group of us going. Our parents got together and bought us tickets. All summer in Europe! Can you believe it?"

Allison was practically bouncing.

Jared held the ticket in his hand.

"But Allison, what about us?"

Allison grew still, her eyes watching him.

"What about us, Jared?"

"I just thought…"

"Jared, it's not like we're engaged or anything. It'll be fun. You can do your thing for the summer, and I'll do mine. We'll both go to State U and…"

"You are definitely going to State U?"

"Well sure. Aren't you?"

"I just thought that maybe we would… you know…"

Allison shrugged. "Maybe we will, Jared. Someday. Or maybe we won't. We're young and we don't have to decide the rest of our lives right now. It's not like we have to get married."

"Allison…"

"Jared, let's just follow the lead of your folks, okay? No commitment, no problem, right?"

"No!" Jared said, but it didn't sound at all like the shout of denial he was hearing inside himself. He felt his world turning inside out.

"It's okay, Jared. Everything will be okay," Allison said with a smile.

She gently removed her plane ticket from Jared's clenched fist and kissed him on the cheek.

The warning bell rang that classes were about to start.

Jared watched as Allison went her own way down the hall and away from him.

Joey lives with Angela and her parents, Mama and Papa. Angela, whom Joey just calls Angela, can be a lot of fun. She brings him candy from her job at the grocery store. She lets him sit on her bed and play with her stuffed animals while she dresses and fixes her hair. Sometimes, she lets Mama take him to the school where he gets to eat lunch with Angela and her friends.

Mama is nice when Angela is not around. Mama likes to hug Joey, and she sings silly songs while Joey helps her with the chores. But when Angela is home, Mama is grumpy. She shoos Joey away and yells for Angela to "take responsibility!"

Sometimes Mama says, "Whose baby are you, Joey?" Then she scoops him into her big, soft arms and holds him close, whispering in his hair, "I'm too old for this baby. I'm too old to be taking care of babies."

Papa plays with him every evening. They build block towers and drive the little cars under and around the furniture legs. Papa doesn't talk much to Angela. Sometimes he tries to get Angela to play, too, but Angela is too busy to build towers and push toy cars. She rolls her eyes at Papa and slams her bedroom door. Joey hates when Angela gets mad at Papa.

Sometimes Papa will sit with a toy car in his hands, rolling his thumb back and forth across the wheels, studying its underside. Joey turns the cars upside down, too. He looks at them hard, like Papa does, but mostly he looks at Papa, from the sides of his eyes, so that Papa can't tell he is watching.

Angela tells Joey that someday they will get a place of their own. She wants to get married so that Joey can have a daddy. Joey isn't sure if he wants a daddy. He knows he had one once. He heard Angela telling her friend about Joey's daddy. He gave Angela five-hundred dollars and told her he didn't want to be hearing about no kid no more. Sometimes, when Angela gets mad at Joey, she tells him to go hide his ugly face. She says his face looks like his daddy, and she doesn't want to see that face no more. Joey wants to disappear when Angela talks like that. He doesn't know how to change his face. He wants a face that Angela likes to look at.

Joey started school this year. He goes every morning because Mama told Angela he needed a head start for kindergarten. Angela is mad about having to drive him every morning, but since Papa agrees to take him on days Angela has to work early, she hasn't made a fuss. Joey doesn't like school. Some kids laugh at him and call him "babytalk," but Joey likes his teacher. Her name is Mrs. Brown. She is pretty and she smells like powder. Joey likes to listen to her read the books at story time. Her voice reminds him of Angela when she is being nice to Joey. He wishes Angela would read him stories.

One night, Papa tucks Joey into bed and tells him not to get bed bug bites. Joey wakes up and sees that his room is full of people. Angela is standing over him. She says, "See my baby? Isn't he precious?" All the girls agree and giggle over him.

One guy says, "Hey there little guy," and a girl immediately begins to gush over the guy and tease him about liking babies. One girl reaches out, touches Joey's face, and pats his tummy. Then they all leave. Angela doesn't say goodnight. Joey can't get back to sleep and he starts to cry. The next morning, his eyes are itchy and his nose is stuffy and sore. He is tired, but Mama says he must go to school anyway.

Sometimes Angela gets mad if Joey tries to follow her or if he asks too many questions. She pushes him away, sometimes so hard that he falls down. If Mama sees this, she yells at Angela. Tells her to grow up. Angela says that it is Joey who needs to grow up. Joey lays on the floor in front of Angela's bedroom door and watches her shoes move across the floor. He likes to listen to her singing or talking to her friends on the phone.

Joey likes to watch TV. Mama lets him watch cartoons every day when he comes home from school. Sometimes he watches TV until Papa gets home. Papa likes to watch the evening news. Papa doesn't like it when Joey watches, too. He says Joey is too loud and sends him out of the room.

Angela brings home movies from the video store. Sometimes she brings home scary movies, and she gets Joey out of bed to watch them with her. They sit together on the couch with a blanket pulled around them, and they eat potato chips and cookies. Joey doesn't like the movies much, but he likes sitting close to Angela. He especially likes it when she throws her arms around him and holds him tightly. Usually, when they watch the scary movies together, Angela lets Joey sleep in her bed and they hold each other all night long. Joey still thinks about the movies, though, and they scare him just as much on the nights he has to sleep in his own bed.

One night, Angela brings home a boy to watch a movie with her. Joey tries to sit next to Angela, but she makes him sit on the floor. The boy starts kissing Angela. When Angela realizes that Joey is watching, she calls him a little pervert and tells him to go to his room. Joey doesn't like the boy who watches movies with Angela.

It is late, and Joey wakes to the sound of Angela and Papa yelling at each other. He can hear Mama crying. Joey tries to understand what they are saying, but he can't make out the words. Angela comes to his room and shoves his clothes into her duffel bag. She grabs his arm so hard it hurts. Joey has to run to keep up with Angela. She holds him so high by the arm that he has trouble making his feet touch the ground and he hits his shoulder on the doorframe as they leave the house. Angela pushes him into a car that is waiting in the driveway. It is dark. Joey thinks that the boy behind the wheel is the same boy who watches the movies.

Angela puts her arm protectively around Joey, and the car tires make a loud noise, like throwing gravel, as the boy spins out of Mama and Papa's driveway. Angela smiles and kisses Joey on the forehead.

"Aren't you happy, Joey? We're going to live in our own place, now. You're going to be a big brother."

Déjà vu

Miranda arrives at my door breathless and big eyed. Her blond curls swirl into something of a bun—loose tendrils dripping and bouncing down the side of her face. Her smile is too much, too many teeth, lips too tightly drawn. That, along with the fact that it is two o'clock in the morning, tells me that something isn't right in her world.

I instinctively cringe when she draws me into her arms in greeting. Here is someone who has stepped beyond the line, someone who has crossed the bounds of good sense, someone no longer grounded by the rules of reason. I can feel it in my core as she squeezes the air out of me.

When she finally releases me, she announces, "I'm leaving."

I stand staring at Miranda, my best friend since the second grade, trying to search for meaning in her face under the light of the dull porch bulb.

"What do you mean, you're leaving?"

"Just that! I'm leaving. I'm leaving Robert and the kids."

I am too stunned to speak.

"I just had to tell somebody."

"You mean you're not telling Robert and the kids?"

"I left a note. But I need to *TELL* somebody," she says, a giggle following the pronouncement.

"You had better come in."

Miranda follows me into the kitchen. I lead her through the room to the breakfast nook where I can pull the sliding glass door and maybe isolate her rantings from my sleeping spouse and children.

"I just need to explain it to someone who will understand," she says.

"And that would be me?"

"Amy, you know me. You understand me."

"The Miranda I know wouldn't leave her husband and kids in the middle of the night."

"It's not like that."

"Not like what? God, Miranda, what in the hell is going on?"

"I just need to tell you, Amy. And you can explain it to them. You can make them understand why I had to leave."

I picture myself telling four-year-old Maggie and nine-year-old Josh that their mother has left them.

"Why would I do that? What could I possibly explain? That you've gone insane?"

"I'm not insane. I'm... I've finally found a way to be happy... truly happy."

"You're not happy?"

"I'm just not..."

"Your children may be pains in your ass sometimes, but you, my dear, are deliriously happy."

"It's just not..."

"And Robert! That man dotes on you. He'd do anything for you."

"That's just it, Amy! There *IS* no me."

"No you?"

"No me! God, Amy, I don't exist anymore. I'm there to clean up after kids and fix meals and..."

"This is about housecleaning?"

"No, I need you to listen to me."

"Miranda, I think you need to start at the beginning."

My friend breathes deeply, and the smile she is wearing fades away. When she looks back at me, her eyes are filled with tears.

"A couple of months ago I joined this mailing list. It was a parenting list... you know, a support group kind of thing. It was people talking about... finding yourself again after giving away so much to your family, to kids. It was really nice... supportive... made me feel like I could do things for myself again. Like there were steps I could take to make my life... I don't know... mine again."

"Keep going," I say. I sit back in my chair and cross my arms.

"There was this guy on there. He always knew exactly what to write. He would respond to every question I posted as if he could see inside me. It was like he knew me. He knew exactly what to say to make me feel better. He even seemed to know things I wouldn't dare post to the list."

She pauses and rubs at the tears that have spilled down her cheeks.

"So I sent him a note—off list—just thanking him for his input and... I told him it felt so nice to have someone who understood me. It was nice to connect with someone. I haven't connected with Robert... I mean, really connected, in years."

"So you started corresponding with him off-list?"

"Well, yeah... I mean... he felt it, too. It was like we were soul-mates or something. We could talk about anything, you know? *Anything*. And we did. We started writing emails back and forth and we talked about all kinds of stuff—politics, kids, books... we have the same tastes in food and everything."

"God, I'm getting a bad case of déjà vu," I say softly, under my breath.

"What do you mean?" Miranda asks.

"Do you remember what you told me after the first date you ever had with Robert?"

"This guy is nothing like Robert," she answers.

"Same tastes in food, you liked the same movies, you voted for the same candidates in presidential elections. This is how you felt about Robert!"

"No, it's not... Robert and I... we don't even talk about that stuff anymore. We haven't seen a movie together in ages."

"Oh please, Miranda."

"But we don't. Robert could care less what I like to eat these days. Robert is so wrapped up in work and the kids."

"And since when is it a sin to be wrapped up in your kids? He's a busy dad who pays attention to them. It could be worse, Miranda. And whatever is going on between the two of you... or not going on... it can be fixed. You just need to take some time together. You need..."

"It's not... it's just that... the kids have become *everything*. There is no us anymore. There is no Miranda and Robert. And there is no me. I've been completely erased."

Miranda's face crumples, and the silent tears that have been falling on her cheeks turn to streams complete with sobbing.

"No one has erased you, Miranda. You are sitting right in front of me, plain as day."

"Bob understands," she gasps.

"Bob?"

"Yeah, Bob. That's his name."

"You're leaving Robert for some faceless voice named Bob that you met on the internet?"

"I have to, Amy. This is something I have to do for *me*."

"And Bob."

"Me. I'm doing it for me."

"No, I don't think you are, Miranda. I think you think you are doing this for you, but I think it's Bob. And I don't think doing it for Bob is any better than whatever you've not been doing for yourself with Robert."

"What?"

"If you can find you with Bob, you can find yourself with Robert. That's where you claim you lost yourself in the first place, right?"

"I thought you'd understand," Miranda says, turning her face away from me, burying it in her hands. "Robert and the kids have swallowed me. I have devoted the last ten years of my life to them and there *is no me* anymore!"

"If that's true, it's your own damned fault, Miranda. If you want more *you*, you've got to *make* more you. It's not something anyone else can take away. And it's not something some guy named Bob can give you back."

"Amy, I thought you would understand. *You* know what it's like to constantly put someone else first. You know what it's like to never get to read a god-damned book or..."

"I know, Miranda, I know. I'm not going to claim I've never felt this frustration."

"Well then…"

"Then bullshit! Miranda! Do you think you're the first mother to ever feel suffocated by her kids? Do you think you're the first wife to ever wish her husband paid more attention to her?"

"Bob says…"

"Bob says! Do you think I give a shit what Bob says? What about Josh? What about Maggie? Think about your kids, Miranda."

"That's just it. I'm *always* thinking about the kids. I think about the kids so much I don't exist anymore."

"I'm not buying it."

"But I don't, Amy! I don't exist outside of them. There is no me left anymore."

"Look, you have time to write notes to Bob? Then you have time to do things for yourself. Redefine yourself if you need to, but don't dump your kids. Don't quit on your family."

"Bob listens to me. With Bob I am human again. I am a person."

"Take that time and find yourself, Miranda. If you can make the time to carry on this online love affair, then you can make the time to do things for yourself. Have you even tried talking to Robert about this?"

"Bob says I should start painting again. Remember how I loved painting, Amy? And I was good—really good."

"Sure. So start painting, Miranda. I bet Robert would even help you build a studio."

"See, that's just it. Robert loves to build, and he's still building things. I love to paint, and I haven't painted in years."

"You stopped, Miranda. That's nobody's fault but your own."

"I couldn't paint with babies and toddlers running around."

"You don't have babies and toddlers anymore. You have a four and a nine-year-old. I am sure they are capable of giving you the space you need to paint.

"I thought you would understand, Amy. You've known me all my life. You know this isn't who I am."

"I'm beginning to see I have no idea who you are."

"But you do. You remember how I was in high school. You remember how I was before I married Robert."

"You were wonderful. And you still are, Miranda. That hasn't changed."

"But it has. I don't have a purpose anymore."

"Then find your purpose. But don't dump your family."

"Where am I left when they are grown and gone? Robert and I have grown apart. The kids will leave home."

"So what, you leave first and spare yourself the pain? That's so noble, Miranda."

"I thought you would understand."

"Yeah? Well, I don't. I think you're crazy. I think you're being stupid and selfish. And if you are going to leave your kids, you are going to be the one to tell them you are going. Don't ask me to do your dirty work for you. I'm not that friend, Miranda. I won't do it."

"I just thought maybe you could help explain to them why I had to go."

"But you don't have to go, Miranda. You may choose to go, but you don't have to do it."

"I have to find myself again."

"If you lost yourself, you are still right here. This is where you lost you. This is where you'll find you. What you're doing? You are running. You are not looking."

"That's not what I'm doing. I just want to give it a try it with Bob. He has a spare bedroom he's going to…"

"Uh huh," I say. I shake my head and put my hand out. "No more. I can't listen to this. You have no idea who this man is. He could be a serial killer. How many women has he lured? I'll listen for the news reports. I'll let them know to check for your DNA, Miranda."

"Amy, he's not like that. God, I'm so sick of those internet horror stories. I *know* Bob. He's my age. He's a little overweight. He's losing his hair. I *know* him and he's not a psycho."

"You know what he's told you. You know what he wants you to know."

"He's telling me the truth. No one could lie that well."

"Okay, okay… so maybe Bob is a good guy. Maybe he's a lonely soul that you've connected with. But that doesn't make this okay."

"I deserve this, Amy. I deserve a chance at happiness."

"You make your own chances for happiness."

"I know! And this is mine!"

"Even if your happiness is going to cost three other people theirs?"

"In the end, it will be better for them. They don't need a mother who feels this way about herself."

"They need a mother."

"I don't know why I came here. I thought you'd understand."

"You came here because you know what you are doing is wrong."

"I'm not wrong."

"You wanted me to talk some sense into you."

"My senses are as clear as they have ever been."

"You need to go home, Miranda. You need to put as much effort into communicating with Robert as you have put into writing those notes to Bob."

"Robert doesn't understand me."

"You haven't give him the chance to understand you. Go home, Miranda."

"I can't."

"Please Miranda, don't do this without thinking about it a little while longer."

"You think I haven't thought about this?"

"I think you're not thinking clearly. Try talking to Robert. Try a month of not talking to Bob, and talk to Robert instead. Just try it and see what happens."

"I can't do that."

"You must."

"I'm leaving, Amy. I beg you, do your best to explain this to my kids."

"I won't."

"I have to do this, Amy. I have to."

Now I'm the one crying. My cheeks are stained with tears.

"Miranda…"

"Amy…"

• • •

The early glow of morning warmed my door as Miranda left. I watched her walk to the end of the sidewalk before closing and bolting the door. Back in the den, I saw the flicker of light from my screensaver.

I clicked the mouse to reveal the content of my screen. My server had long since timed-out and booted me off-line. The note on the screen read:

JUSTAFELLOW: I can't tell you how much I look forward to meeting you here each evening.

AGAL: I know. I can't wait to get the kids in bed and have to stop myself from jumping for joy when John takes his book up to bed to read.

JUSTAFELLOW: It's like we are soulmates. The understanding runs so deep.

AGAL: Hold on, someone is at my door. I'll be right back.

JUSTAFELLOW: Is everything okay?

JUSTAFELLOW: I'm just surfing and waiting for you to come back...

JUSTAFELLOW: I miss you...

JUSTAFELLOW: I think I'll head to bed now. Hope everything is okay. Same time tomorrow?

I shut my email program down and wait for the computer to stop humming as the screen flickers to black.

Upstairs, I peek in on my slumbering daughters. The morning light is cast so beautifully across their tiny blonde heads. My son, in the next room, slumbers soundly. His gentle snores remind me of his father.

In our bedroom, my husband lazily opens his eyes at the sound of our door.

"Please don't tell me you are just now coming to bed," he says as he stretches and pulls the blankets up to his chin.

I smile and go to sit on the edge of the bed. He glances at me warily, tentatively reaching his arms to encircle my waist.

"Everything okay?" he asks.

"It will be," I sigh deeply and bend to kiss his forehead. "Want to talk?"

"Sure. You bet I do," he says.

"Good," I answer. "That's good. And everything is going to be okay. I promise. Starting today. We're going to make everything good."

A Paperback Life

"Aurora Hemingway – Acquisitions and Classification," the nameplate on the desk says.

No one ever comes into her office. It seems rather silly to have a nameplate on her desk at all. Aurora supposes the nameplate serves as a reminder to her superiors that "Aurora Hemingway" is her name.

"You know Aurora; she is the woman who stays late working *every night*, the one who never speaks," she overheard her boss saying to the acquisitions librarian.

"Aurora is the mousey brown-haired woman with the bun, the one whose terrible thick glasses make her eyes seem eerily large." That's the way the cleaning staff had been describing her one night, not realizing she was just on the other side of the partition, able to hear every word.

These are the things Aurora overhears when others do not realize she is close enough to be listening, which is often.

As Aurora examines the engraving, it occurs to her that the nameplate serves as a reminder to herself, as well.

"I am Aurora Hemingway," she whispers.

Aurora pushes at her heavy glasses with the back of her hand. She gathers her books, reading material for the evening, and layers them into the backpack she likes to call a purse. Looking at the nameplate one last time, she says, firmly and with conviction, "Aurora Hemingway."

She fumbles with the keys when she gets to her car. It takes her a moment to get the door unlocked. Once she has the key in the ignition, she sits a moment, reflecting. Her lover will be waiting for her at home. She smiles, imagining how Luca will greet her at the door, his well-tanned skin glistening from perspiration worked up cooking over a hot stove. His golden locks will spill over his meaty shoulders. Luca will draw her to him and kiss her deeply. Remembering his thick, Italian accent, she wonders what gourmet cuisine he has prepared for her tonight.

She closes her eyes and hears him say it: "Vermicelli in marinara sauce, for my love."

Luca is a former Mr. Universe and designer of his own line of exercise apparel. He is also a master chef. Aurora met him while in Italy attending a book conference. It was love at first sight.

The gas gauge on Aurora's little yellow compact never falls below three-quarters of a tank. She always enters the store, pays with a ten-dollar bill, and then goes back outside to pump the gas into her tank.

The red dress she wears today matches the color of Luca's roadster. Maybe Luca will drive the sporty car tomorrow when he picks her up after work—she'll have to leave early again—and takes her to watch the ballet. After, they will drive to a secluded area in the mountains and make passionate love.

Aurora jumps when the gas pump clicks loudly, signaling the tank is full.

She returns to the store where the clerk has her change waiting for her on the counter, along with a lottery ticket, the numbers randomly picked by the computer. She scoops the change into her purse. She searches in her wallet for last week's ticket and goes to the display of winning numbers.

"Any matches this time?" the clerk asks.

"No, not a one," Aurora says, sighs, and leaves the store.

Phoenix, her black and white cat, meets her at the door, mewing loudly. Aurora picks him up and goes to the refrigerator.

Stroking his head, she says, "Tuna, beef, or chicken?"

A partially emptied case of each flavor, canned tins of cat food, fill the bulk of the refrigerator. A carton of milk, bottle of ketchup, and a months-old container of yogurt complete the ensemble within.

Aurora selects a can of tuna from a case and deposits it and the cat on the counter. She peels the lid back and leaves the cat to enjoy its meal.

"Vermicelli in marinara sauce," she says, returning and pulling open the freezer door.

Aurora pulls out each frozen container and briefly studies the contents; veal parmesan with steamed vegetables, chicken chow mein, Cajun style black beans and rice, three-cheese lasagna... Locating the Italian cuisine near the bottom of the stack, she peels the top back and pops it in the microwave.

Aurora plucks a paperback book from the top of the stack in her bag. There he is, on the cover, locks of golden hair, a smile to win all hearts, and rippled chest muscles glistening with perspiration.

Aurora begins to read.

> Spent from hours of making love, Luca and Aurora lay clinging to each other, knowing that at any moment, Aurora's husband might return. It has only been by luck that their affair has been left undiscovered, so far. Aurora no longer loves her husband, of course, but Jack is a strong-willed, possessive man who refuses to see reason and let her go.

The microwave dings. Aurora pulls out her meal, stirs it with a fork, and eats as she continues to read. It is nearly eleven o'clock when she becomes Mariana, a wealthy socialite who is about to find true love with the stable boy, Gus. Mariana falls asleep, feeling the powerful horse beneath her as she and Gus race across the meadow to their destinies, and to each other...

dedicated to Astrid Lindgrin
and any child who ever loved reading the adventures of
Pippi Longstocking

Way out at the end of a tiny little town was an old overgrown garden, and in the garden was an old house. Well honestly,
it was hardly recognizable as a garden these days, but Tom and
Annika remembered a time when it *was* a garden, and therefore,
though it was now no more than overgrown weeds and sapling
trees whose seeds had been allowed to sprout and flourish in the
long-neglected fertile soil, they thought of it as a garden in all its
lush and wild glory. Years before there had been people living in
the old house. Tom and Annika had vague memories of an old
man and woman who had tended the garden daily. More clearly,
however, they remembered a visitor to the garden. That was many
years ago when they still considered themselves children. Her
name, though Tom and Annika had often debated the accuracy of
this particular memory, was Pippi.

Pippi was the granddaughter of the old couple who had once
occupied the house. At least, that is what Tom had surmised in the
years since that splendid summer they spent with the delightful
playmate right next door, her hair, the color of carrots, standing
wild and unruly from her head. Annika was more prone to fantas-
tical stories of Pippi's origins. Pippi had been an orphan, Annika
liked to remember. Her father had been lost at sea, and her mother
had long before gone up to heaven. But Tom overheard his parents speak of the children of the old couple numerous times over
the years. The son, he was fairly certain, had been Pippi's father.

For years Tom had watched the empty old house with longing.
At seventeen, it was mere habit more than anything. He no longer
believed that the girl, Pippi, would one day appear on the front
porch. He scolded himself every time he sat on the stump of the
tree in his own back yard, wondering about the fate of the girl he
barely believed existed. Pippi had become his measuring stick,

however. Every girl he met, every girl he contemplated asking out on a date, could not hold a candle to the whimsical, wonderful girl he had dreamed about the summer he was ten.

Surely she had been a dream, had she not? Tom questioned his memory for the umpteenth time. All he had now were faded letters—LANGSCHRIEBER—on a mailbox at the end of a drive that led to an old abandoned house.

On Saturday, the first official day of summer break, Tom found himself lying awake in bed, listening to the sound of a lawnmower. It took him a moment to realize that it could not be his own father mowing the lawn. It was Saturday morning and his parents were religious about their routine this time of year. They took their morning run together—they would complete six miles on a Saturday—and then returned home to shower, dress, and eat a healthful lunch of salad and sandwiches before heading to town, not Lindgren, where they lived, but Wahrstadt, farther down the road.

Tom stood up and stretched, stumbled into his bathroom to splash water on his face, and made his way down the stairs. Annika was at the kitchen window looking out toward the house next door.

"Somebody is mowing Pippi's lawn," she said in her bubbly cheerleading voice.

Tom and his sister had gotten on quite well as children, but more and more he found himself annoyed by Annika. Especially since she had been voted head cheerleader for the upcoming school year, a feat unheard of for a junior at Lindgren High until Annika came along.

He shrugged his shoulders, but sidled up alongside his sister anyway, and stared out toward the old vacant house. A white truck had parked at the end of the drive. An enormous riding lawnmower had apparently been delivered on the truck's flat-bed trailer. The driver wore a brimmed hat, not exactly of the gardening variety, and what appeared, for the moment, to be a very clean white shirt.

"Maybe someone is moving in." Annika was bouncing on the tips of her toes as she spoke.

"Maybe," Tom grunted, moving to the refrigerator to find himself something for breakfast. He located a drumstick from last night's dinner and held it between his teeth while pouring himself a tall glass of milk. He drizzled chocolate syrup into his cup from the sticky, overturned bottle in the door and fished for a spoon in the silverware drawer to stir with.

"You animal," said Annika with disgust as she glared at him.

He pulled at the chicken bone with his teeth and chewed with his mouth open. Annika rolled her eyes, and her lids fluttered as she huffed and turned her back on him. He slurped his milk loudly, leaning close to her as they both watched the action in the yard next door through the open kitchen window.

Tom burped purposefully in his sister's ear.

"You are disgusting," she exclaimed and stormed out of the kitchen.

The window cleared for viewing, Tom pulled out a plate and some napkins and took his breakfast to the kitchen table. He watched the man on the mower with interest. The machine zigged back and forth, back and forth, with precision strokes, gradually clearing a strip of lawn about a quarter of the entire width. Tom's attention was drawn to movement at the house. There were two men that he could see, both of whom seemed to be moving in and about the first story of the home. They were removing boards from the windows and taking measurements for glass panes that needed to be replaced.

After a half-hour of watching, Tom couldn't contain himself any longer. He took the steps of the stairs two at a time back up to his bedroom. He pulled a ball of socks from the drawer and pulled his faded blue jeans from the clean laundry pile on the chair at the end of the bed. After a bit of deliberation, he settled on an old blue t-shirt at the bottom of the pile. He slipped it over his head, pulled on his shoes, tied them quickly, and darted down the stairs and out the door.

A bit of a run and a leap found him hurdling the fence that separated the two yards—the nicely kempt yard of Tom and Annika's family, and the overgrown Langschreiber garden. Tom slowed his pace as he approached the house, not wanting to seem overly eager or aggressive. Once on the dilapidated porch, the house really didn't look as bad as it did from the view in his yard. He needlessly rapped his knuckles against the frame of the open door. The workmen had already caught sight of him and were raising their eyebrows in expectation.

"How can I help you young sir?"

Tom stifled a smile at the man's formal tone.

"Actually, I was wondering if I might help you," Tom replied carefully. "Looks like this place could use an extra hand or two." Tom gestured widely, peering into the gloomily lit room that he had entered only once before in his life. It had been packed with furniture then. It was a warm little house, even if a little… unique. Pippi herself had invited him in, and though he had met no adults, he had not honestly believed her claim that she lived there all alone. After all, he'd seen the Langschreibers tending their garden, day-after-day, for as many years back as he could remember. He had also not believed that the noises coming from the back room were made by Pippi's pet monkey. He had glimpsed a figure through the doorway and, even though Pippi swore that the monkey wore clothes, Tom was sure it had been much more the size of, perhaps, a small man.

"Well help we could use, yes sir. But you'll have to be talking to Mr. Nilsson about that you will."

"Mr. Nilsson?" Tom questioned, taking the odd tongue (Pirate was the word sprung into his head) in stride.

"Aye, Mr. Rutherford Nilsson would be the man to be speaking to. He's riding the mowing machine out front, he is."

Tom dropped his head in a quick jerk of understanding and retrieved his hand before allowing it to fly to his forehead in salute.

"Thank you. I'll go have a talk with him," he said as he backstepped to the edge of the porch. He jumped the three steps down and jogged the long path that was once a driveway toward the monstrous machine that was brazenly chopping through weeds and small trees as if they were merely wisps of dandelion. He waved when he was close enough to catch the driver's attention. The roar of the engine immediately slowed to a purr and the whirring blades stopped. A tiny man in a starch-white shirt dismounted. His hat? Tom had worn one like it when the Lindgren High Choir sang in barbershop style for a spring program two years before.

Most amusing was the man's tidy little black bowtie, secured neatly at his neck.

Tom paused with dawning recognition.

"Why, if it isn't young Tommy," the man laughed heartily, a surprisingly deep voice for his small stature.

"Mr. Nilsson?" Tom felt he knew the name at once, and not just from moments ago when the men at the house had directed him to the little man on the lawnmower.

What Tom remembered about the man, he couldn't quite pinpoint, but the memories were surfacing, nonetheless. Tom found himself smiling brightly, and he cringed a bit with embarrassment at the excitement that seemed to be welling from within.

"Tommy boy, call me Rutie, please. No need for formalities between old friends."

"Old friends," Tom found himself shaking hands heartily with the little man, searching deep in his mind toward a picture taken when this man was taller, more imposing, yet wearing—could it be the same?—starch-white shirt and tidy-black bowtie.

"You've grown up, young Tom. I shan't be surprised, I suppose. But you truly have, haven't you? All man now, not a lick of boy in you, is there?"

"Yes, Sir." Tom felt the blush rise in his cheeks, still not sure if he was remembering real life or drawing from a childhood dream.

"I would love to stand and chat, son, but there's much to do, much to be done."

"I thought maybe I could help," Tom added quickly, more determined than ever to put himself to work.

"You're free to work?" the little man asked.

"I am, Sir. School is out for the summer and, well, I haven't gotten a summer job yet. I was going to take it easy. Pick up odd jobs here and there. I'll be a senior this year, and I figured it might be the last free summer I have."

"Ah, a senior it is, is it?" Rutie rubbed his chin thoughtfully. "Well I can't pay you much, but extra hands are always appreciated. Can you start today?"

"I can start right now," Tom said. He felt giddy with anticipation.

"Well, then, why don't you pull that truck up closer to the house? There are tools in the back and the garden is in need of some attention.

Tom grinned despite himself, nearly skipping to the truck. A million questions popped into his head, like fireworks on the fourth. He grasped at them and sorted them into categories—filling in memories of fact as well as fiction. Mr. Nilsson had been a friend of Pippi's, he was sure. But even before he met Pippi, he had known Mr. Nilsson. Perhaps he had been the Langschrieber's gardener? More than that, Mr. Nilsson had been a friend. Tom remembered him small like a child, but not as small as Tommy had been. He was a grinning man with a boisterous laugh. He grilled hotdogs. He kept Tom's mother in stitches with stories of... the high seas.

"Pirates," the word came to Tom again, and he muttered it under his breath as he darted back to his own yard to get work gloves from the shed.

Annika caught Tom before he'd had the chance to cross the fence between the yards again.

"What are you doing?" she inquired.

"Some gardening," he answered, flashing her a beaming smile he hadn't shared with her in years.

"What for?"

"Just to help out," Tommy said, feeling anxious to get to work. "It's Mr. Nilsson."

He paused for a moment and turned back to his sister. "Annika?" he asked. "You do remember Mr. Nilsson, don't you?"

Annika wrinkled up her nose in thought for a moment, then her eyes grew wide as she drew in her breath.

"Mr. Nilsson!" she gasped. Giggles followed. "Mr. Nilsson, of course! He was Pippi's monkey!"

Tom shook his head. That was exactly the image he had been struggling with. Mr. Nilsson, the monkey. Clearly, that had been just a fanciful bit of play they must have engaged in years ago when they were children. Mr. Nilsson was a man. An odd and funny man, perhaps, but a man no less.

Annika surprised Tom by crossing the fence between the yards with her own rake and hoe in hand, their mother's work gloves on her slender white hands. "Tom, why do you think our memories of that summer are so fuzzy?"

"We were kids. It was a long time ago."

"But it wasn't so long ago, Tom. It couldn't have been more than seven, maybe eight years ago. We both remember Pippi, but we can't even agree that Pippi was actually her name."

"It wasn't Pippi. I'm sure of that. Her parents called her something else. She had a long, elegant name," Tom said while raking hurriedly, creating neat stacks of weeds and leaves in a row at the edge of the garden.

"She didn't have parents," Annika argued.

"Of course she had parents," Tom scoffed. "That orphan bit, it was just a story of Pippi's. She was always telling stories remember? Her stories were… magical."

Annika wiggled her nose and politely sneezed. A second sneeze came more forcefully, and she had to pause to blink her watery eyes and sniffle the third one away.

"You really shouldn't be out here, Annika. All these weeds are going to stir up your allergies. You're going to be sick in bed with a headache tomorrow. That's no way to start a summer."

Annika shrugged. "But I want to. It's nice to be outside in the air and the…" she sneezed ferociously, three times in a row.

Tom watched her blink and struggle not to rub her eyes. "Go get a washcloth at least. You can wet it in the faucet and keep your face cleared of dust every little bit."

Annika grudgingly agreed to the wisdom of Tommy's suggestion. He watched her trudge toward home and stop to balance herself through another series of sneezes on the way.

When Annika returned, face freshly dampened with a handkerchief tied up around her nose and mouth like a mask, she attacked a stand of weeds with a vengeance. "Why are they fixing up the house now, Tom?" she asked. "Who is moving in?"

Tom looked toward Rutie, who had nearly completed mowing the second quarter strip of lawn. "I didn't ask," he finally answered.

Annika watched her brother, her brow furrowed. "Wouldn't it be cool..." she bent and exposed a line of bricks with her gloved hands.

"It's the path," Tom said as he dropped his own rake and knelt to help Annika pull back the undergrowth. "It's the garden path!"

The two knelt together, rubbing the dirtied golden bricks with their gloves.

"Oh Tom," Annika said, breathless. "Let's make it beautiful again. Do you remember how beautiful it was, Tom?"

"I do," he whispered, "I do."

In the days that passed, the garden began to resemble order once again. The siblings spent three full days clearing the garden of brush and weeds and another two on their hands and knees, weeding and turning the soil of the long abandoned flower beds. In places there were still flowers, wild in their blooms and color. At the end of the first week, Rutie provided them with an allowance to replenish the garden. They planned a trip to a large greenhouse in Wahrstadt.

To the delight of their parents, Tom and Annika were getting along as well as they ever had as children. They came home exhausted each evening, but continued to wake early each morning. As Tom fell into bed each night he found himself dwelling on questions he had still not asked. Why were they working so hard to restore the fallen home next door? Who was coming to Villa... What had Pippi called the old house? Villa.. Villekulla?

Tom smiled as he drifted off to sleep, to think that a humble home in the humble town of Lindgren would be dubbed with such a pretentious name. Tomorrow he would ask Mr. Nilsson... Rutie.

He would ask Rutie what all the hub-bub at the old house was really about.

It was Wednesday when Tom and Annika stood in the center of the garden, a rainbow of color blooming at their feet, the polished stone birdbath awake with fresh water, already attracting resident robins proudly cleaning their puffy red breasts. Their parents had come for a tour.

"Well done, kids. You've really done some incredible work here." Tom's father spoke with stern authority.

"That they did, sir. That they did," Rutie said, approaching from the direction of the house where the workmen—two more had joined the original pirate duo—were priming for paint.

"Rutie!" Tom's mother greeted the man with open arms. "It's so wonderful to see you. We were surprised when Tom told us you were back."

"It's wonderful to see you too." Rutie kissed Tom's mother on each check, bringing a blush to her handsome face. He then grabbed Tom's father by the shoulders, pulling the taller man down for a similar greeting. Tom's father, discombobulated a bit by what he must have deemed an inappropriate show of affection, responded, nonetheless, with an enthusiastic handshake.

Tom found himself grinning, enjoying the show of his parents made uncomfortable, yet seemingly entertained, by this little man.

"I believe you were traveling the world seven times over, was that the plan?" Tom listened eagerly as his father engaged Rutie in conversation.

"Well… seven times, six times, five, four … the world is so full and there's no covering it, truly. I lost count. But I have been enjoying myself," Rutie straightened his bowtie. It occurred to Tom that the white shirt remained as clean and unwrinkled as it had on the very first day.

"So what brings you back?" Tom's mother queried.

"Oh, you have not heard?" Rutie raised his eyebrows in wonder.

"We've heard nothing, not even a rumor."

Rutie looked to Tom and Annika who shrugged their shoulders without answer.

"Yes, well, perhaps I haven't shared the news." Rutie seemed to be searching his memory for confirmation. "The boys are here. I supposed everybody knew. There are Langschriebers coming back to the Villa."

"There are?" Annika practically squealed.

"Of course. Who else?" Rutie crossed his thin arms and rocked back and forth on his feet, his expression wandering to focus on another place or time.

"I didn't realize there were any Langschriebers left," Tom's father said.

"Oh yes, there were four, in fact, until just recently." Rutie lowered his chin to his chest and made the sign of the cross. "The son who grew up here, he and his wife met untimely deaths in the mountains of Nepal."

"Oh my." Tom's mother raised her hand to her mouth and shuddered.

"It was a terrible tragedy," Rutie said with a sigh. "But an adventurous one, no doubt. And how better for a Langschrieber to go than in the throngs of an adventure?"

The parents nodded wisely as if they understood completely.

"So who is left?" Annika asked quietly.

"The granddaughter and her spinster aunt, technically not a Langschrieber, but accepted into the fold years ago when it became obvious that she was cut from the same cloth. She has been sailing, the aunt, on a boat up the Amazon River. I hope that we have caught up to her by now, and I believe that she and Viki will be arriving any day now."

"Viki?" his sister spoke the question Tom longed to ask. Tom felt his chest sink with disappointment.

"Yes, the granddaughter, Viki."

Tom fretted with the spigot on the birdbath. He started to ask about the other granddaughter, Pippi. Whatever had happened to the girl with the carrot-red hair who had graced their lives so briefly once upon a time? But with sudden sureness, Tom turned his back on the group in the garden. There had been no Pippi. She was a figment of imagination, the combined efforts of he and his sister a lonely summer so many years ago. Maybe he had been old enough to understand. Maybe she had been a creation, his last act of childhood before he crossed that border where the imagination no longer reigned. A surge of disappointment welled in his chest. Tom felt his breath catch. He excused himself rudely from the group in the garden and made his way toward his own yard, now an easy task with the freshly mowed lawn. He leapt the fence and rushed into the house. He hauled his tired, aching body into the shower.

Scrubbing every last speck of dirt from his skin, working to erase the nearly two weeks of effort he'd put into the soil next door, he finally stepped from the shower when the hot water had turned lukewarm. He toweled himself dry and shuffled into his bedroom, sinking into his freshly cleaned bed, silently thanking his mother for the day she had spent washing sheets and changing bedding.

Tom slipped into slumber almost before closing his eyes. He was vaguely aware of the footsteps of his sister and his parents ascending the stairs to their own bedrooms later that night. He slept through the night and on into the daylight, conscious of the risen sun, but unable to pull himself from the weight of sadness that blanketed him. Refusing to greet the day, he slipped in and out of consciousness through a world of active dreams. He was watching a girl who rode a galloping white steed. Or was it just the white mule that the Langschrieber's once housed in their back yard? She could walk on her hands quite amazingly. Tom giggled in his sleep, watching her feet dangle above her head, kicking in rhythm to keep her balance. She had been there, but only briefly, and Tom and Annika had missed her so much that they had continued, in their imaginations, to join her in play. She had been real, hadn't she? And he had started the routine of watching the house next door, through the news that the old couple had died while abroad, the gang of men who had come to board up the house, the grass that grew long and took over the once well kept yard.

It was nearly noon when he made his way down to the kitchen. His parents were sitting at the table, discussing an article in the latest *Time* news magazine. His sister was watching wistfully out the window, peeling an apple in slow motion. She turned to him and smiled, wrinkling her nose at him. Pinned to her blouse was a butterfly-shaped brooch that caused Tom to catch his breath and stare in wonder.

Annika glanced down and shrugged her shoulders. "I think it was from Pippi," she mused. "I found it in my jewelry box this morning, the one shaped like a tiny piano that you gave me when I was little, the one that plays rag-time tunes when you prop up the lid. I had forgotten it was there." *The wings of the butterfly were set in blue and red and green stones.* She waved her hand in Tom's face. I think this was from Pippi too. On her pinky finger was a small ring with a green stone.

Tom turned and dashed back up the stairs. In the back of his closet he found an old cigar box. He tore off the lid and dumped the contents out onto his bed. He sorted through the contents; some polished rocks, a lucky rabbit's foot, an eagle feather, a chain of pull tabs collected from soda cans… and there it was, a broken knife handle, mother-of-pearl, the sharp edge of the blade long gone. As well, he found an ivory flute.

He sat on the bed, gingerly rotating the flute between his fingers. He brought it to his lips and blew gently. A sweet whistle pierced the air. He felt goosebumps explode across his arms, traveling up to the nape of his neck. He took a deeper breath and blew slowly. The sound pierced the air again, this time deeper and more sustained. The curtains from his open bedroom window fluttered. The sounds of an engine running traveled the distance from the drive next door. He glanced out to see a white pickup truck pulling slowly up to Villa Villakulla. He pronounced the name aloud as if to test it.

The pickup came to a full stop; the trailer being towed behind it creaked loudly. Tom watched as a woman departed the driver's side of the cab. Her hair was dark and cropped short. She was stout, but not heavy. She walked to the trailer and stepped up on the runner, sticking her arm in as if to assure some wild beast within. Tom heard the door of the passenger side open without registering the significance of a second inhabitant. Then the sun sparked brilliantly, and Tom heard himself gasp. A second woman had departed the truck. Her hair was distinctly red, not so much the color of carrots, but the deeper shade of the finely bottled wine his parents drank when they had guests.

Tom watched the redhead move toward the trailer, unhitching a latch that held the back gate. Rutie appeared at the door of the old Langschrieber house, gaily calling out to the new arrivals. He embraced the dark-haired woman with a kiss on each check. He rushed to the end of the trailer to the redhead, who seemed to be torn between releasing the beast within from its cage and greeting the little, eager man. The two embraced, kissed cheek to cheek and cheek to cheek again, and then hugged mightily, a shriek of laughter escaping the girl that matched the pitch of the ivory whistle in Tom's hands. He blew once more on the whistle, gently, so softly it barely made a sound.

Rutie pulled the gate of the trailer wide open while the girl entered. Within moments, she emerged leading an enormous white horse. It followed her as they made a wide circle around the truck. Two of the pirates… workmen, Tom corrected himself, came out of the house and hurried around the side, opening a gate in the back fence for the woman and horse. The girl walked without hurry, apparently speaking kind words to the horse as they walked past the house. She looked out into Tom and Annika's garden as she led the beast past. Then, as if she felt him looking down upon her, she looked up into Tommy's window. A broad smile crossed her face and she waved up at him. His hand waved back of its own accord. Could it be?

As the girl walked the horse to the small barn near the back of the fenced lot, Tom leapt to his feet and darted into the hallway. His sister met him midway on the stairs.

"Tom! I think it's her! It's Pippi next door. She's got red hair. She's got a white horse. I think it's Pippi, Tom, I really do!"

Tom grinned at his sister, and together they tromped down the stairs. They burst out the door of the house, and then slowed their steps simultaneously, holding each other back by pulling on one another's elbows.

"Just be cool," Tom whispered to his sister.

"Be cool yourself," Annika said, giggling with delight.

"No really, she's just a girl," Tom scolded.

"No really, this is Pippi we're talking about!"

"We don't know that it's Pippi," Tom cautioned.

"Who else would it be?" Annika replied.

The two of them crossed the fence together in as dignified manner as they could muster. The red-haired girl was returning from the barn area, followed by one of the pirates. Tom checked himself mentally to learn the workmen's names so that he wouldn't embarrass himself by calling them pirates out loud.

The dark-haired woman had entered the house with Rutie, who waved joyously from the door. Tom and Annika stood at the edge of the flower garden, not wanting to appear too eager as she approached them. The girl smiled with a broad mouth and very white teeth. Her small nose, the shape of a potato, was dotted all over with freckles. Tom found her face familiar, yet much matured and... lovely.

She approached them with her arms outstretched. Tom prepared himself for a handshake, but felt himself being pulled toward her, and she kissed his cheek on each side. "Tommy," she said his name without hesitation. "Annika!" His sister was given the same warm greeting, only Annika hugged back with a fervor that Tom could not muster.

"It's wonderful to see you both again," the girl said. Her diction was formal, and without the odd accent of the pirate workers.

As if knowing the pair would follow, the redhead made her way into the garden to the circle of stone benches that Tom and Annika had carefully cleaned of grime just days before. The girl, for now Tom could see that, though womanly, she was still as much a girl as he was a boy, sat and looked up at them with expectation.

"So?" she queried brightly. "Tell me what you've been up to? Tell me how you've been?"

Tom and Annika simply looked at her, open mouthed.

"Pippi?" Annika finally managed to squeak.

"Oh," the girl giggled and waved her hand as if brushing away a pesky fly. "Nobody's called me that in years."

"But you are Pippi?" Annika repeated, finally sinking to a seat on a stone bench.

"Well actually, I've gotten rather accustomed to going by my real name these days, Viki." She winked at Annika and patted the remaining bench, motioning Tom to sit down.

She smiled, her broad mouth taking up more of her face than one would expect from her otherwise fine features and petite stature. "What?" she looked directly at Tom. "You look as if you don't believe me."

Tom opened his mouth, but found himself without the words to speak his mind.

"I see you've still got the whistle." Pip… Viki gestured to the ivory flute in Tom's hands that he only then realized he was still holding. "And the butterfly and the ring."

Annika nodded vigorously.

"And I still have the music box," Viki hummed a tune. "I've taken it with me everywhere."

Tom could hear the tune in his own head now. He could even picture the music box, a spare gift his mother had kept on hand just for occasions like last-minute birthday invites. He felt a bit ashamed, at this memory, that he and Annika had not specifically chosen a gift for Pip… Viki's birthday.

"Well, I hate to run you off so soon. But I'm bushed. It's been a grueling day. A grueling couple of weeks now that I think of it. I'd like to settle in and get some rest. Besides, you can't come back if you don't go home, right?"

Viki stood with these words and clapped her hands together. She reached boldly toward Tom and grasped his hand. She wrinkled her nose in an adorable fashion as she spoke her parting words.

"Viki P. Langshreiber. You do remember me, don't you, Tom."

"Of course," Tom managed to stutter his first true words of the meeting.

"Well good. We'll see each other tomorrow then? We've got a lot of catching up to do."

Tom felt dizzy as he watched her go. He looked at his sister, and felt like his mind was waking to a dream he'd had years ago. "Her name was Pippilotta Delicatessa Windowshade Mackrelmint Ephraim's Daughter Longstocking," he said. "How does one get Viki out of that?"

High School Reunion

The last time Kelly sat on this wall she was seventeen years old and holding a cigarette in her hand. The cigarette had come from Colette, the mother of a boy, Kelly's first crush. Colette was thin and sexy, something Kelly had been led to believe women gave up when babies came along. Kelly loved the way Colette looked when she threw back her head and laughed, red lipstick and black wavy hair causing every head in the vicinity to turn and stare. Kelly also loved the way the orange tip of the cigarette drew attention, giving her the spark she always felt she lacked.

A song by the Beatles had been playing from the edge of the practice field on somebody's car stereo. Kelly hummed along softly, wondering if there was any truth to the wisdom she'd been gleaning from the lyrics of the songs by John, Paul, George, and Ringo.

A car of rowdy teens had driven by. A horn blared.

"Only freaks and geeks still listen to the Beatles," somebody yelled.

Kelly remembered this line particularly well because she took it as a compliment. She had pulled the cigarette to her lips with confidence and somewhat inhaled, and even though the smoke clawed at her throat, she managed to slowly blow it back out in that smooth and even way that Colette did right before she would wink and say something profound.

Kelly had liked being considered part of a community larger than herself. Just because the people she spent time with had not fit anywhere else in the scheme of school cliques, it didn't mean that her chosen friends could not also roam as a pack, a hodgepodge of free and lonely spirits. Andy Berger was a really good basketball player, for instance, but he also liked to wear eye makeup and the jocks didn't especially appreciate him off the court. Sandy Demowitz was a cheerleader until junior year. She remained cute, bouncy, and athletic, but unwilling to conform enough to maintain inclusion in the extra-cheericular activities. And then there was Colette's son, Howie, who seemed impervious to the fact that the most popular kids in school would love to have had him exclusively at their weekend parties, and oblivious to the fact that his latest girlfriend was a card-carrying wallflower. No one, not even the loners Kelly hung out with, had known the girl's name before Howie started dating her.

More than twenty years later, her first and last experience smoking remains a top memory from her high school years. Kelly can still imagine herself with cigarette in hand. She is one of the few from her crowd to show up for the reunion. It is rumored that Howie will be here, as well, but being the one person from the Risdell High Class of 1987 who had actually made a name for himself in the big wide world, Kelly doesn't figure he will head immediately to his old hangout. He likely won't think to look for her at all.

It is true that Kelly had somehow managed to age more like Howie's mother, Colette, than her own. Momma had been the very definition of frumpy housewife until she died of breast cancer ten years ago. There had been a couple of years after the birth of child number three that Kelly had grown curvaceous to the point of having dimpled thighs, but at thirty-six she had run her first half -marathon and could still wind her thirteen-year-old son playing one-on-one in the driveway. A full marathon was on the agenda for year forty.

How confident and far removed she feels from that girl who sat on this wall twenty years ago, pretending to smoke a cigarette.

The roar of the crowd inside gets louder. Kelly turns her head to better listen.

"I am not meant to be here," she whispers. "What a lie," she says a little louder. "I should be at home with my kids tonight."

The patio brightens when the gymnasium doors open. The noise coming from inside roars for a moment before the doors fall shut again. A man steps out and begins searching in his jacket pocket. He pulls out a cigarette and starts to light it. The flame from his lighter flickers and goes out prematurely.

"I'm sorry," the man says. "I didn't know anyone else was out here."

He steps closer, as if contemplating taking a seat on the wall beside her.

"I don't mind," Kelly says. "I don't mind at all if you smoke."

"Thanks," he says and leans against the wall beside her. "These things are crazy, aren't they? A bunch of adults gathering to relive the so-called glory days, as if the acne and hoping some girl would agree to kiss you beneath the bleachers was something you still aspired to."

He wordlessly offers Kelly a cigarette. She accepts.

He turns and looks her in the eye. "You don't look like a smoker," he says, his eyes travelling down to take in her well-toned arms, her narrow waist, and her athletic hips and legs. He takes the cigarette back, lights it for her, and returns it to her hand.

"So, are you the wife of a Risdell ex-jock or ex-scholar?" he asks.

"Neither," she laughs, pleasantly surprised by how deep and Colette-like her voice sounds. "How about you?"

"Isn't it obvious?" he says, strutting forward, pulling at the lapels of his sports jacket like a runway model. "I am the one-and-only, third husband of the Class of 1987's head cheerleader, prom queen, and mostly likely to still be struggling with an eating disorder."

"Tricia Collins? You're Tricia's husband?"

"The eating disorder give it away?"

"No," Kelly says. "I didn't know." She shakes her head.

"Of course you didn't," he says, inhaling deeply, the tip of his cigarette glowing fiery red. "You are one of those wholesome, good girls. I can tell. You always assume the best of people."

"Oh really..." she starts to say, but he quickly cuts her off.

"So you know Tricia?" he asks. "From the ten-year, I suppose. You are one of the long-term Risdell Raven spouses?"

She turns her head away and fakes a draw from the cigarette. He seems to accept her silence as agreement.

She asks, "And how about you? Scholar or jock? On your own turf."

He starts choking and Kelly watches him, concerned for a moment until she realizes he is laughing. "Me? Neither," he gasps. "Hell no."

He hikes up the front of his pants so far she can see the outline of his balls at the crotch. He slouches, pushes his front teeth out over his lower lip, and schlepps away, dragging his feet across the pebbled concrete.

"No," she says and laughs. "No way."

He turns around and squints at her, pushing up imaginary glasses. He sniffs, runs the back of his hand across his nose, and scratches his ear before shuffling back to where he started. He sticks his hand out in stiff greeting. "M-m-m-my name is Anthony. M-m-m-mitchell. Siebert. The th-th-th-third." He pulls his hand away and wipes at his nose again, then grabs her hand firmly and shakes it up and down, his head bobbing in time.

The uber-nerd fades and the charming man she's been talking to leans casually against the wall.

"I was voted most likely to still be living with my mother," he says.

"What happened?" she asks, still laughing.

He shrugs. "I slept with an older woman who took pity on me the summer after my freshman year in college. Let's just say she schooled me on how to dress and what to say. She encouraged me to start doing my own laundry and to move out of my mother's place. Once I realized I was just a project, and I managed to put my heart back together … girls started seeing me in a different light."

"I bet it was fun going back to your class reunion," Kelly says.

Anthony shrugs his shoulders. "Never been," he says, studying the ground as if something compelling were there. "Never will."

The gymnasium doors open again and the two of them squint against the glare of lights. A woman in three inch heels and a sleeveless white blouse trips toward them. Kelly would have recognized Tricia Collins anywhere. From a distance, she is as beautiful as she had been in high school.

"Anthony! There you are," Tricia sings. "Why is my trophy husband hiding out here?"

The man opens his arms wide and embraces the blond. "Tricia," he says when she releases him. "This is…" He quiets, looking puzzled for a moment before he furrows his brow.

The woman peers into the semi-darkness at Kelly's face.

Anthony blinks. His mouth remains open as if the introduction has been plucked from his tongue.

"It's okay," Kelly says. "I didn't actually introduce myself. I'm Kelly. Kelly Taylor."

Tricia's eyebrows furrow. "Kelly?" she repeats. "Kelly Taylor?"

"Wait a minute. *You* are a Risdell Raven," Anthony says.

"Huh?" Tricia's face puzzles into a frown.

"She is," Anthony says. "She's in your yearbook. Class photo section. Page 47. Second row from the bottom, starting from the left: Chance Symmonds, Charles Taggart, Destiny Tann, Kelly Taylor, Sioban Trent."

"Hmm." Tricia continues to ponder.

"I'm not good with faces," Anthony says. "But photographic memory; I remember everything I read."

Kelly slides off the wall and smashes the cigarette into the ground with her shoe. She turns and leans against the bricks, looking out onto the darkened practice field.

"Yeah, I was a Raven," she says. "At least, in body."

She turns toward Tricia who is still looking at her through half-closed eyes, her head cocked to one side.

At least this much is familiar. A classmate had actually asked Kelly's name at graduation, claiming he had never seen her before, though they'd had three classes together in high school alone, and several more in junior high before that.

Tricia finally shrugs her shoulders in defeat. "Nope. Don't remember you." She turns toward her husband, reaching up with one long finger and tapping the side of his nose with a lacquered

red nail. "Howie Starr has arrived, Dear. I would like to introduce you."

Kelly's heart turns a little flip-flop in her chest. Howie was her one and only reason for coming to this reunion.

Would he remember her?

Once, in the ninth grade, Howie Starr had held her hand in the back of a car at the drive-in. They had shared friends, though Kelly had never really considered Howie someone she knew. Thanks to their common social circle, their paths had sometimes crossed. Once, they kissed under the mistletoe at a Christmas party. It wasn't a real kiss, not a big kiss, but a lovely kiss as Kelly remembered it. Howie had looked at her for a long time, and she had somehow managed to maintain eye contact. And then he had stepped forward, pointed at the mistletoe hanging over their head, and firmly, but sweetly, placed his lips on hers. She had melted in that instant. Perhaps even fallen in love. But the moment passed too quickly and a rowdy group of boys had called Howie away. Someone spiked the eggnog at that party. Kelly had stayed and sang Christmas carols until she was hoarse, but Howie did not look her way again.

Howie Starr had always been no more, no less than friendly. He said hello when others simply passed her by. Howie smiled at her in the hallways between classes, though he rarely called her by name. Once, Kelly had looked up from her lunch tray to find Howie Starr staring at her from three tables over. When she smiled in return, he had ducked his head and started eating. She watched him for a long time, but he never returned the look.

Kelly watches as Tricia leads Anthony back to the gymnasium.

"It was nice to meet you, Risdell Raven Kelly," he calls over his shoulder.

Tricia seems to have already forgotten she is there.

The blare of noise from inside the gymnasium fills the air once more and Kelly's shadow is cast, temporarily, long out onto the football practice field below.

Kelly straightens her shoulders and takes in a big breath of fresh air. A swift breeze picks her hair up off her shoulders and tosses it about. She pictures Colette. She lifts her chin. She wills herself the confidence to join her classmates at the reunion.

Inside, the scene is very much a reflection from twenty years before. A handful of individuals move rhythmically near the basketball free throw line on one side, hips swaying to the same music that played over the loud speakers when they were many pounds lighter and not yet worried about things like crow's feet and thinning hair.

A larger crowd is spread along the sidelines and clustered around tables of food and drink. Groups of three and four sit at varied spaces along the bleachers on the far side of the gym.

Howie is easy to spot. He stands near the punchbowl, bordered by the largest cluster of Risdell Ravens in the room.

"It's not about who you were," Kelly says under her breath. "It's about who you are."

As she moves forward, the crowd parts. She smiles at several familiar faces and makes an effort to speak the name of each face she passes. "Hey, Kelly!" Voices in the crowd sound back, surprising her.

"How are you, Kelly?"

"It's Kelly! Guys. Hey, it's Kelly Taylor."

She stops to embrace a few whose faces move her to something of wistful remembrance. Natalie Tipton had the locker next to hers through four long years of high school. Erica Rathke played clarinet almost as poorly as Kelly had, but always had a smile and friendly word for everyone she met.

Kelly knows, however, the precise moment Howie sees her, and she lets her gaze stray no longer. He stops speaking, and the entire crowd around him turns to look. Kelly has never felt so visible.

Howie steps forward when she smiles at him. He comes toward her and his arms encircle her tightly. The next thing she knows, her feet are being lifted from the ground, the result of a bear hug of monumental proportions. When Howie lets her down, his face is still buried beneath her hair. He speaks so softly that she is the only one who can hear, though everyone around them has stopped talking and is clearly listening, as well.

"Kelly Taylor," Howie says. "You are the whole and only reason I came to this reunion, and I was about to decide you weren't going to show."

Kelly feels the blush rise in her face. She wants to run, but his arms hold her securely in place.

"Howie Starr," she answers, feeling every eye in the room upon the two of them. "I hardly imagined you would remember my name."

Howie releases her and they take each other in for a moment. Kelly knows she has changed little, though the power to turn heads had grown some as she had gotten older. Howie's face, so common on movie posters and gossip magazines in grocery store checkout lines, is so well-known to her that the real thing standing here in front of her seems somehow less than authentic. He is more human, perhaps slightly less beautiful, than the Howie Starr she has grown to know so well on the theater screen.

"Please tell me," he says, "That you are single and looking to kindle a romance with an old friend from high school this weekend."

Kelly remains silent, thinking about her kids. She lets her mind wander, for a moment, to their father, the man she would always love.

"I came to see what all of these near-forty-year-olds had done with the last twenty years of their lives," she finally says.

Howie sighs and says, "I expected nothing less." His eyes remain on hers with full attention.

"But..." Kelly says.

She does her best to ignore the fourteen-year-old girl inside her mind who is doing a happy-tap dance.

Howie is listening.

"But?" he repeats.

"You are my..." Kelly can't bring herself to say it out loud. She feels the heat rise in her cheeks. "You are on..." She tries again, and it finally comes out as a whisper. "You are on my freebie list."

She manages to watch Howie's face, though maintaining eye contact is beyond her capability.

It takes a moment, but Howie finally grins in comprehension.

"I am the celebrity you can have sex with without consequence?"

"Well, one of three," Kelly says and bites her lip and nods.

"Of course," Howie says. "The list always has three. Does your husband know we went to high school together? Is he here?" Howie looks around as if he might recognize her husband.

"Yes," Kelly says. "And no. He's not here, but he knew, yes, that we went to high school together."

"Did he know you were coming to the reunion?" Howie asks. "Did he even wonder? Worry? That I might be here?"

That had been the discussion once upon a time, of course. The freebie list had been made all in fun. Tom had originally vetoed Howie Starr.

"No way," he had said, as the game had almost turned into a real argument. "You went to high school with the guy. I'm not going to risk visiting your parents for Christmas only to find out that Howie Starr, your celebrity freebie, is staying at the end of the block with his mother!"

But when he'd gotten sick, it had been Tom who said, "You know who you should go look up when I am gone? Howie Starr. That movie guy. You deserve a star, Kelly. You deserve…"

"You will be my shining star forever, Tom," she had answered, shushing him.

"Kelly?" someone is touching her arm. She pulls herself out of her dream-like state. Howie Starr remains about ten feet away, talking with Deryk Matthews, the valedictorian of their class. Not all brains, that boy. He was athletic *and* attractive. His hair had thinned considerably, but Kelly would have recognized him anywhere.

"Is everything okay?" the wife of another classmate asks, her warm hands reaching out to cover Kelly's.

Kelly smiles and nods. "I'm good. Everything is okay."

Someone from behind her says, "It's been twenty years. He shouldn't still have this effect on me," and it occurs to Kelly that she was probably not the only girl in high school who had dreamed herself someone potentially special in Howie Star's enigmatic eyes.

"Oh come on. It's Howie Star. He has that effect on everyone," another woman says. Kelly can't identify if she is classmate or spouse.

Kelly looks around, trying to find someone familiar with whom to anchor herself.

"Shall we grab some drinks and go find a spot on the bleachers," she asks, rather randomly addressing the crowd.

She recognizes her freshman lab partner, James, and he and his wife agree. They are soon joined by Natalie and Erica and a half-dozen others whom Kelly remembers as friendly kids in high school.

She almost doesn't recognize Sid, who had been a six-foot beanpole when they graduated. He had at least tripled his width and was now quite handsome. Kelly suspects he had grown accustomed to turning heads in the intervening years since they received their high school diplomas.

She begins to relax and enjoy the visiting, so many names she has not thought of in years. Even a few of those whom she would have said were strongly embedded in their cliques in school stop and say hello.

"Can you believe this all used to be so hard?" Erica asks the growing group on the bleachers. "I would get up at five in the morning just to prepare myself for a day of high school."

"Holy cow, five AM?" someone answers. "My coping response was to sleep as much as possible. My mother always had to drag my ass out of bed and kick me out the door to get me to school before first bell rang."

"Oh god. I had to ease into it. If I just woke up and rolled right off to school, I'd suffer stomachaches all day," Erica says.

"But you were always so friendly and cheerful," Kelly says. "I always assumed school was easy for you."

"Academically easy, maybe," Erica says. "But the social stuff nearly killed me."

Kelly wonders why she and Erica had never bonded in high school. They'd been friendly enough, she supposes, but she finds herself wishing she could go back and give her high school self some tips.

Imagine if she'd had true friends in high school. Imagine if she had taken the time to communicate with those whom she had been forced into daily contact.

As the evening wears on, Kelly keeps half an eye on Howie Starr, and then begins to lose track of him. She eventually stops wondering if Howie is going to look her way. She ceases obsessing over whether he recognized her.

It is well past midnight when the reunion crowd begins to thin.

Kelly is tired, but in a blissful way. She has caught up with people she had nearly forgotten existed. She has laughed about the antics of old biology teachers, and reminisced about the most beloved English teacher, as well as complained about the least loved economics class. It is late when she collects her things and leaves through the gymnasium doors. She takes one last look to the wall where she had spent so much of her youth. Howie Starr is standing there, alone, looking out over the practice football field.

She hesitates so slightly that she barely recognizes herself. She redirects from her path toward the parking lot. Howie turns toward her as she approaches. He smiles and lifts his chin in recognition.

"Kelly Taylor," he says. "And here I was beginning to think that this whole reunion was going to pass while the only girl I ever regretted not asking out in high school snubbed me and ignored me."

She looks around, searching for confirmation that Howie is real and standing right in front of her. Her impulse is to pull out her phone, to call Tom, to run this by him. The thought passes in a flash as she remembers that her husband is gone.

Howie smiles, and she thinks that he must be real, but when she doesn't say anything, his chin drops. He lowers his gaze to the ground. She thinks maybe the color in his cheeks pinks up a little.

Kelly hears footsteps from behind. She turns to see Anthony and Tricia making their way to the parking lot. Anthony waves and winks. Kelly waves back.

Tricia, bless her heart, calls out, "It's Kelly Taylor and Howie Starr!"

"Howie Starr," Kelly repeats, turning back around to face him. "I hardly imagined you would remember my name."

Howie smiles and shakes his head. "How could I ever forget?"

"Please tell me," she says, feeling the troubled years of childhood surrender to the boldness of her current life. "That you are single and looking to kindle a romance with an old acquaintance from high school this weekend."

"I had hoped for nothing less," Howie says.

I Wasn't Scared

*Mrs J. = Phyllis Jordan

The house moaned and whined as it shifted into a restless sleep. The trees scratched on my windows and the moon glistened in the sky, submitting a steady yellow beam onto my carpet. Despite the icy drafts in my quarters, I got up and walked to my window. I stood shivering as I gazed out into the night. Except for the howling of the wind, all was silent. Because of the many trees, the only thing I could see was the barn, a homely barn with its rotting rafters and dusty cobwebs which hung everywhere. The barn had probably once been beautiful when it was new. Now all that was left of the red paint was little splotches here and there. The sliding doors had fallen off their hinges long ago and now lay on the ground leaving somber holes in the side of the aging barn. I disliked the barn from the beginning. Something evil lurked there. I could feel it every time I went near. Something was warning me to stay away. It haunted my dreams and tried to frighten me every time it had had a chance. It wanted to fight a battle, and it was determined to win.

I sat up in bed with a startling jolt. What had wakened me? The barn, it was calling me to come. It wanted to scare me. I hurriedly put on my garments and rushed outside. As I neared the barn, I slowed, for it was watching me, waiting for me to come so it could devour me. I knew it wouldn't harm me though, not yet. It was like a cat who liked to play with its mice before the final blow. I wasn't scared, not the first time, nor the next. I entered one gradual step after another. I jumped, startled by a large rat that scampered across my path. I ambled in and out the hallways, looking into the stables and other tiny cubicles that were spaced sparingly throughout the barn. Shadows danced in the corners, and at times I would hear footsteps behind me, though nothing would be following. Ghostly laughter rippled through the hallways, echoing, trying to confuse me, but I wasn't scared, not that time, nor the next.

I didn't enter the barn again for many days. When I did, I was prepared, and before I could get three feet from the entrance, the old, broken down door swung back onto its hinges, locking me inside. I ran to the door screaming and pounding, only to discover it was no use. I would never get out. I turned to look around and saw large bubbles had covered the wall. Grotesque blisters that became larger and larger began to cover my hands and legs. Little grey worms began to pop out of them and squirm all over, sinking themselves into my skin.

That was the first of a series of events that happened in the barn. But never once did I get scared. I knew what it was trying to do, drive me crazy, but it couldn't because I wouldn't let it.

I don't remember how I finally got out the second time, but I returned two days later. This time I was going to win. Remember, the barn didn't scare me. It tried, but it never succeeded. I think I could have won if it weren't for those people who came and interfered. They came and got me and wouldn't let me finish the battle. They'll pay, though. They'll be sorry they didn't let me finish.

As I walked into the barn for the last time, I was prepared for any strange events that might occur, but the barn didn't fool around this time. It beckoned me to the hayloft. It was ready to kill the mouse. But I was prepared and knew I couldn't lose. If only they hadn't stopped me, I could have won. The loft was empty except for a couple of hay bales stacked in one corner. A creature about four feet high approached me, dribbling foam from his mouth. He had small, sharp ears and eyes that quivered and twitched. He walked in a hunched over manner, his lengthy arms almost dragging the ground. I could feel the heat from his body, and I knew he was the one I was going to fight. He just stood and glared at me, but I wasn't scared. The battle began. I had trouble keeping up with him at first. He would dart from corner to corner, ceiling to floor with the quickness of a panther and the agility of a gymnast. He didn't fight fair, but I never once got scared. I knew I would win. He slapped me from wall to wall. I got in a few good hits myself, but mainly I stayed up by wit. I was smarter than he and found I could baffle him by making loud noises and surprising him.

Then they came. They came in their white jackets and shoes, strapping me into a bed and ignoring my pleas to let me finish the battle. As they took me away, I could hear the barn laughing. It was laughing at me.

White is such a dull, boring color. Everything here is white. Even my jacket, which has no opening for my hands, is white. They sewed the arms to my shoulders. They think I am crazy and they tell me I'll get better. But I'm going back to finish the battle. I'm not scared.

The End

Credits

- An earlier version of "Glorious" received third place in the short story category of the 2005 Kansas Authors Club Literary Contest (www.kansasauthors.org)

- "The Circus Boy" was published in *The Flint Hills Review*, 2016.

- "Charade" received an Honorable Mention nationwide in the Half-Price Books Short Short Bedtime Story Competition, 1995.

- "Virtual Farm" was published at *Page and Spine* (www.pagespineficshowcase.com), August 2014.

- "In America" was published in Kansas City Voices in 2007.

- "In America" was an Honorable Mention in the 2006 Kansas Voices Contest, Winfield Arts Commission.

- "Jared Loves Allison" won second place short story under the title "In Their Own Way" in the 2001, District 7, Kansas Authors Club Writing Contest.

- "The Substitute" won second place short story in the 2016, District 2, Kansas Authors Club Writing Contest.

- "I Wasn't Scared" was selected by Phyllis Jordan, Dodge City Junior High English and Journalism instructor, to be entered in the Kansas Authors Club youth writing competition, 1984.

Acknowledgments

I first must thank the members of the Emporia Writers Group for giving me a place to touch base with other writers each month. Thanks also to Rick Becker and the Cicerones at Mulready's Pub for creating such a lovely place for the likes of our group (and others) to gather. Thanks to all the many movers and shakers in the town of Emporia, while I am at it, for creating such a lovely place to live and dream and be inspired by other folks who take pleasure in living and dreaming, as well. Everywhere I turn, there is a strong spirit of "can do" in Emporia, and I am happy to apply my part to nurturing and growing our literary community.

Special thanks goes to Hazel Hart (hazelhart.com) whose superb editing skills give me the confidence to publish this collection of short stories that has been written across the decades.

Extra special thanks goes to Cheryl Unruh, my dedicated writing buddy, soul sister, cheerleader, pet sitter, and often provider of whatever else I might be in need of at the moment.

To properly thank my family would require another 186 pages of words, so I will simply say that they are the best. Rand, Evie, Maddie, Kaman—thanks for being my inspiration and, so often by example, for pushing me to do more, try harder, and be bolder.

Tracy Million Simmons
Emporia, Kansas
May 2017

About the Author

Tracy Million Simmons enjoys writing about the people and places of her home state of Kansas, both real and imagined. Her writing resume includes more than 500 articles in print, from feature articles in national and niche publications to ghostwritten material for busy health professionals. She is a 17-year, multi-district member of the Kansas Authors Club (www.kansasauthors.org). Tracy is a past mini-fellowship winner from the Kansas Arts Commission and has received an honorable mention in the Kansas Voices contest (Winfield). She is the author of *Tiger Hunting*, a 2013 J. Donald Coffin Memorial Book Award winner, and one of three authors of *Green Bike, a group novel*. Tracy is the founder of Meadowlark Books, an independent publisher that focuses on stories and authors from the heartland. Learn more about Meadowlark and its authors at www.meadowlark-books.com.

TracyMillionSimmons.com
facebook.com/TracyMillionSimmons/

Illustrations

Also by TMS

Tiger Hunting, a novel
Chasing Tigers Press—April 2013
A J. Donald Coffin Memorial Book Award Winner, 2013

When Jeni returns to her childhood home in western Kansas, she never imagines that she'll be hunting a white tiger escaped from the circus or competing with an ape for the affections of the boy she once loved. While she waits for the man she's left behind to notice she's not coming back, she reconnects with her family and works to pick up the pieces of her life.

Green Bike, a group novel
Meadowlark Books—September 2014
With authors Kevin Rabas and Michael D. Graves

Green Bike follows the lives of three couples, using the McGuffin, or shared symbol, of a classic Schwinn bike to link parallel tales. Following these tenuously linked tales, Green Bike is at once a muted romance, a graduate school bedroom romp, and a love letter to a dying mother.

Praise for *Tiger Hunting*

Tiger Hunting, a novel, by Tracy Million Simmons
a 2013 J. Donald Coffin Memorial Book Award Winner
Chasing Tigers Press, March 2013
ISBN-10: 1482687011
ISBN-13: 978-1482687019

"When a story begins with large circus animals spread across a Midwestern highway as *Tiger Hunting* does, you know that author Tracy Million Simmons has one heck of a tale in store for the reader. Jeni is on her way back home to Kansas from Texas when she spots a dolphin on the side of the road. The reason for Jeni's visit to Kansas is her younger brother's graduation, but inside the trunk of her car reveals that she has left her boyfriend James, who unfortunately doesn't seem to notice or care that she's gone. After coming to the conclusion that she has simply been playing the role of follower in her own life, Jeni helps in the search for the tiger on the loose. On her search she realizes that she too has been lost for quite some time and vows to find herself, as clichéd as that might sound.

The most unexpected thing about Tiger Hunting is just how funny it is. Never mind that a tiger is on the loose, but relationship discussions with a cheeky ape called Orville kick the hilarity up a notch. Tracy Million Simmons has quite a unique voice and a flair for description, propelling the reader right into the heart of western Kansas and Dodge.

Filled with gypsies, bearded ladies, overbearing parents and renewed friendships, Tiger Hunting is a uniquely entertaining look at what it can really be like to go home again. The fast pace of the book will have you laughing along as Jeni and a wacky cast of colorful characters continue to search for the elusive tigress."

~ Natasha Jackson for Readers' Favorite

"Tracy Million Simmons's *Tiger Hunting* captures the remote world of Western Kansas; its rugged people and terrain, its young people's hopes and parents' dreams. Set in and around the fabled town of Dodge City, the author weaves a compelling story of a twenty-something's unexpected homecoming in a penetrating study of one of life's most tenuous moments. Anyone who has been thrown off the marked trail, or felt compelled to run away to join the circus, will identify with this novel. Today's "Boomerang Children" need a safe place to come home to, to reflect, retrace steps, find a new path. Perplexed parents who make room for their boomerangs may discover that they're the ones with something to learn about the modern world. *Tiger Hunting* explores modern family life in a fast-paced, humorous, and well-crafted read that plunges deep into the heart of the heartland. As the hunt roared to its dramatic, hopeful climax, I couldn't put it down."

~ Grant Overstake, author of *Maggie Vaults Over the Moon*

"*Tiger Hunting* was expertly written, and very enjoyable. I loved Jen and her struggles, and I love the setting in western Kansas. I was captivated by the narrator and her struggles and appreciated the metaphorical references to two strong females striving to find their own ways in the world. Jeni was a fascinating character, one of those fictional people I would welcome as a friend."

~ Ann Fell, author of *Sundrop Sonata, a novel of suspense*

WWW.MEADOWLARK-BOOKS.COM

Meadowlark Books is an independent publisher, born of a desire to produce high-quality books for print and electronic delivery. Our goal is to create a network of support for today's independent author. We provide professional book design services, ensuring that the stories we love and believe in are presented in a manner that enhances rather than detracts from an author's work.

We look forward to developing a collection of books that focus on a Midwest regional appeal, via author and/or topic. We are open to working with authors of fiction, non-fiction, poetry, and mixed media. For more information, please visit us at www.meadowlark-books.com.